A VILLA IN SICILY:

CAPERS AND A CALAMITY

(A Cats and Dogs Cozy Mystery—Book Four)

FIONA GRACE

Fiona Grace

Fiona Grace is author of the LACEY DOYLE COZY MYSTERY series, comprising nine books; of the TUSCAN VINEYARD COZY MYSTERY series, comprising seven books; of the DUBIOUS WITCH COZY MYSTERY series, comprising three books; of the BEACHFRONT BAKERY COZY MYSTERY series, comprising six books; and of the CATS AND DOGS COZY MYSTERY series, comprising nine books.

Fiona would love to hear from you, so please visit www.fionagraceauthor.com to receive free ebooks, hear the latest news, and stay in touch.

BOOKS BY FIONA GRACE

LACEY DOYLE COZY MYSTERY
MURDER IN THE MANOR (Book#1)
DEATH AND A DOG (Book #2)
CRIME IN THE CAFE (Book #3)
VEXED ON A VISIT (Book #4)
KILLED WITH A KISS (Book #5)
PERISHED BY A PAINTING (Book #6)
SILENCED BY A SPELL (Book #7)
FRAMED BY A FORGERY (Book #8)
CATASTROPHE IN A CLOISTER (Book #9)

TUSCAN VINEYARD COZY MYSTERY
AGED FOR MURDER (Book #1)
AGED FOR DEATH (Book #2)
AGED FOR MAYHEM (Book #3)
AGED FOR SEDUCTION (Book #4)
AGED FOR VENGEANCE (Book #5)
AGED FOR ACRIMONY (Book #6)
AGED FOR MALICE (Book #7)

DUBIOUS WITCH COZY MYSTERY
SKEPTIC IN SALEM: AN EPISODE OF MURDER (Book #1)
SKEPTIC IN SALEM: AN EPISODE OF CRIME (Book #2)
SKEPTIC IN SALEM: AN EPISODE OF DEATH (Book #3)

BEACHFRONT BAKERY COZY MYSTERY
BEACHFRONT BAKERY: A KILLER CUPCAKE (Book #1)
BEACHFRONT BAKERY: A MURDEROUS MACARON (Book #2)
BEACHFRONT BAKERY: A PERILOUS CAKE POP (Book #3)
BEACHFRONT BAKERY: A DEADLY DANISH (Book #4)
BEACHFRONT BAKERY: A TREACHEROUS TART (Book #5)
BEACHFRONT BAKERY: A CALAMITOUS COOKIE (Book #6)

CATS AND DOGS COZY MYSTERY
A VILLA IN SICILY: OLIVE OIL AND MURDER (Book #1)
A VILLA IN SICILY: FIGS AND A CADAVER (Book #2)
A VILLA IN SICILY: VINO AND DEATH (Book #3)

CHAPTER ONE

"You've done it again, Concetta!" Audrey Smart said, checking out the wound her mentee had dressed on an injured Labrador. "This is perfect."

"I know!" the model-pretty brunette said, finishing up the stitches and giving the animal an affectionate pat. "I love sewing. My stitches have always been the neatest."

"I couldn't have done it better myself," Audrey admitted. "Now, we just have to—"

"I got it," she said, reaching for the gauze before Audrey could.

"All right, but—"

"I know, I know, keep the wound clean," she said, reaching for the antiseptic. "It's all under control. This is easy-peasy!"

It was. Concetta Busillo, Audrey's new second-in-command at Mussomeli, Sicily's new veterinary center, was only a year into vet school, but she was already proving to be a very quick study. Not only was she young, beautiful, and fashionable, like a model who'd just walked off the pages of a magazine, but she was also capable, and had the confidence to match. It was almost intimidating. But after quite a lot of growing pains and working herself to the bone, Audrey had to admit that having her here was a big relief.

Plus, Concetta was fluent in Italian, a big help, since in her four months on the island, Audrey hadn't quite gotten the language down yet. As a local, too, she'd given Audrey a good dose of the culture and history of the town.

Yes, Audrey could safely say that Concetta was a lifesaver, and hiring her was one of the best decisions she'd made since moving to Mussomeli.

Not that she'd made many of those. It seemed like everything good she got out of her life, she did it the hard way. Nothing ever seemed to come to her easily.

"I think it's time to lock up and go home," Audrey said with a yawn.

1

Concetta nodded. "Oh. I just want to check in for tomorrow's appointments and make sure we're all ready. And this place could use a little scrubbing, don't you think?"

"Yes. That's . . . great." Audrey hadn't thought of that. Being a vet in this town, with the massive stray problem, she'd gotten used to being *reactive*, rather than proactive. Concetta clearly liked to plan ahead. It was a good thing.

But as much as Audrey tried to push the feeling away, she couldn't help the tendrils of envy that creeped into her mind. Being a supervisor and owner of her own clinic, the one calling the shots, was new to her, and just about as foreign as the island she now called home. *She* was the one who was supposed to be making those important decisions to keep the place running.

They finished washing up and Audrey looked over at her young protégé. After only a week, Concetta had become almost indispensable to her. She was way more together than Audrey had ever been, when she was that age. In fact, the young woman could probably have run the place on her own, like clockwork.

Which only made Audrey feel a bit . . . unnecessary. When she'd moved here, this had felt exciting. Like a challenge. And now that everything was under control, the challenge seemed to be gone.

Oh, stop it, Audrey. You're the vet here. She looks up to you. And she's amazing. There's still a lot to be done with the stray problem in Mussomeli. You'll get the challenge back. And you're just feeling low because of what happened with Mason.

Yes, a week's time had done nothing to mend the tear in her heart.

She cringed as a thought came back to her. Mason Legare, the man she thought she loved, standing at his front door, gorgeous and speechless, tail between his legs.

Forcing those thoughts away, she said, "Then you can lock up?"

She nodded. "Sure. I think I'll also straighten out that supply cabinet in the back. It's not very neat and we don't want anything going missing."

"Okay," Audrey said. What was wrong with the cabinet? She hadn't even noticed that it was messy. "Sounds goo—"

"You ever think of cataloging everything online and checking things out as they're taken? That way, when something is out of stock, we'd know it right away and could automatically reorder."

"Uh . . . no," she said. Truly, she'd had so much else on her mind. "But that's a great idea. I'll put you in charge of that."

2

As she went to gather her things, more thoughts of Mason intruded. He'd been the main thing on her mind lately, and every time she thought of him, she got a little sick to her stomach. A week ago, she'd been so sure her fellow American expat, lured to Sicily by the one-dollar home promise, was fated to be her one-and-only. He'd been so sweet to her, doing little things for her vet practice and for her, fixing the place up with his carpenter skills, providing her homecooked Southern meals.

Last week, she'd realized it had been Mason all along. She'd run to his house, more certain than ever. In fact, she'd wanted to scream it from the rooftops. *I love Mason Legare . . . and I think he loves me, too.*

With that thought firmly in her head, she'd rushed off, so fast that even her pet fox, Nick, had had trouble keeping up with her. She'd dashed past her house at the corner of the *Piazza*, down another drive, to *via Milano,* and didn't stop until she'd arrived at Mason's front door. As usual, the place was awash in light.

And it had felt so right, to be standing there in front of him. So excited was she to see him again that she'd flown up all three steps in one leap and knocked on the door.

He'd opened almost at once, and the smell of something delicious hit her. He had a dishtowel slung over his shoulder, like he'd just been cleaning up, and was wearing little wire-rimmed spectacles. She blinked. He looked like a sexy Harry Potter. His first reaction was delighted surprise, which morphed into something she couldn't quite understand. Something uncomfortable. "Hey!"

He'd looked over his shoulder, as if hiding something. And he *was* hiding something. Something big.

It was mortifying, now, to think how she'd begun to babble, about how sweet he was and how she really wanted to tell him everything on her mind. Her face had been heating, and his seemed to heat right along with it. Right then, she didn't know why.

But now she knew. He'd been embarrassed for her. She grabbed her purse from the hook on the wall of her office, and cringed again at the thought of what had happened next with Mason. That *woman.*

"Mace, who is it?" a female voice had called from inside.

Before Audrey could register what was happening, the door had been pulled wider, and standing in the way was a dark-haired bombshell. She was tanned and toned and lithe and every supermodel's worst nightmare. "Hi . . ." she'd said flatly, her gaze shifting between the two of them before landing on the soup in her hands. "Are you delivering food? You must have the wrong address. We already ate."

"Um, no, I just . . ." She looked over at Mason, who said nothing. He did nothing, too. Just allowed her to stew in her humiliation.

She'd made up some excuse about how she was thanking him for fixing her mold problem, and started to back away.

"Mold? Gross," the woman had said, flipping her long hair over her shoulder. "Macey, I'm going to take a bath upstairs. Okay?"

Macey?

He didn't answer her. Instead, he'd just continued to stare at Audrey, a guilty look on his beautifully kissable face.

It was all Audrey could do not to burst into tears. Instead, she'd rushed back home and consoled herself, alone, with a bowl of soup.

In fact, she'd been consoling herself with *a lot* of bowls of soup lately. Soup, and some of the most decadent of Sicilian delights—arancini, risotto, and lots and lots of pasta. This morning, she'd had trouble buttoning her jeans. After only a week of moping, she'd already gone up one pants size.

Yes, it was safe to say that Audrey was in a bit of a slump. Almost thirty-five years old, she felt like she was spinning her wheels, both in her career and her love life.

Maybe Mussomeli is a mistake. Maybe I should go home.

That thought had occurred to her many times over her four months in Sicily, but never so strongly as it did right then. Yes, escape would've been nice, if she had something back in the United States to escape to. The fact was, she'd left Boston to escape the exact same thing—a dull and dead-end career, a go-nowhere love life.

And maybe that was the worst feeling of all—that no matter what she did, she couldn't escape that fate.

The phone rang as she was heading for the door. Concetta could have let it go straight to voicemail, since office hours were over, but always willing to go the extra mile, she picked it up. "*L'ufficio di Dottore Smart,*" she said, patiently and efficiently. "*Si.*"

Audrey hovered at the door, waiting to see if she was needed, and she was. Concetta looked up and raised a finger to her.

One moment, she mouthed. "*Si. Qualcuno parla inglese? Dottore Smart parla solo inglese.*" Pause. "*Si.*"

She handed the phone to Audrey and said, "Someone who says he is from Lipari."

"From where?" Audrey's sense of geography had never been good.

4

"It's an island. North of here."

"Island? What do they want with me?"

She laughed. "I don't know. They want to speak to you. I told them you only speak English."

Audrey took the phone. "Hello?"

"Dottore Smart?" a heavily accented voice said. "Are you the veterinarian in Mussomeli we have heard much about?"

She blinked. "I don't know. What have you heard about me?"

There was a chuckle. "We hear that you have done a great job with the stray problem in the town. Yes?"

"Well, I've been trying," she said, happy to know her work was helping. Mussomeli's stray pet population had been a bit of a nightmare, but little by little, it seemed to be getting better. Just a few days ago, Councilman Falco had stopped by to tell her the rest of the council was noticing an improvement, and they were pleased.

"I'm Matteo Gallo. I'm on the town's council, and the mayor has charged me with seeing what we can do with the problem of our stray cats."

"Cats?"

"Yes. We have too many, they are becoming a nuisance. Mayor Ernesto Bianchi is requesting your presence here on the island."

Audrey's eyes widened. She looked at Concetta, who mouthed, *What is it?*

She mouthed back, *How far away is Lipari?*

Now, Concetta's eyes were wide. "Pretty far. Like six hours. Plus you have to take a ferry."

"Hello?" Gallo said over the line. "Did I lose you?"

"No, I'm here!" Audrey spoke into the phone. "I was just trying to find out where Lipari was. It's quite a ways from here."

"Yes, yes. We're about half a day's travel away. So we'd put you up for a few days in our lovely town. In that time, you can see what we have in place right now and make recommendations for us for the future. Would you be amenable to that?"

"Well, I have my practice here, and it needs me."

"I understand. But we're desperate. It would only be a few days. And I promise, you will be well compensated."

Audrey frowned. She'd been putting a lot of the renovations on her house and the clinic on credit, and she'd only just begun to pay them off. So the money was definitely tempting. But what would it say to the town, to Falco and the rest of her new customers, if she picked up and left so soon?

"I'm sorry. I don't think I can leave the practice. It's just so new."

"I understand, but please. You are the only one who can help us. If it's a question of money, just name your price."

She laughed. "It's not a question of money. It's my clients. They—"

"We will pay you handsomely. Very handsomely. We need you here, *Dottore*. These animals are suffering."

Her breath left her. She never could stand to hear of animals suffering. But what about the animals here? She looked over at Concetta, unable to force her mouth to form any response.

Concetta stood up, concerned, and rightly so, because Audrey felt faint.

Finally, Audrey choked out, "Well, I can see . . ."

"Please do. We'd love to welcome you to our island, as soon as you can make the trip."

She gripped the phone in her sweaty hand. The instinct was there, to jump at the offer, but this vet center needed her, too. They'd just gotten a litter of kittens in, and the bunnies they'd saved a few weeks ago were going to need to be homed. There was just so much to think about. "I wonder . . . could I have twenty-four hours to think it over?"

"Oh yes. Of course. I'll give you my number."

Audrey sat on the edge of the reception desk, grabbed a pen, and wrote down Matteo Gallo's information. When she hung up, Concetta said, "What was that all about?"

"They want me to consult with them about their stray problem. It seems very dire. It'd only be for two days, but—"

"If the animals need you, you should go!"

"They didn't mention how much money, but it would help me pay off my bills for renovating this place, for sure," she said, tapping her finger against her chin. "But no. I can't. This place needs me."

Concetta shook her head. "I think we will be fine for two or three days, barring any emergencies."

"But what about those new kittens? The bunnies?"

"They're fine. I live right down the street, remember? And I can get Luca to help me. Plus, I can see to any of the check-ups and regular appointments," she said, looking over the schedule. "And that's all we seem to have for the next week."

"Yes, but—"

"I can handle it!"

Audrey hesitated. *Are you trying to push me out?*

She hoisted her bag onto her shoulder and went to the door. "I'll have to think about it."

She went outside and passed through the middle of town, with its quaint, narrow streets, lined with charming old buildings with colorful shutters and wrought-iron balconies. The town was bustling. As the sun set behind the buildings, people moved about the busy sidewalks, and some called *Buonasera* to her. The evening was warm and pleasant. It was a lovely place to live, but Audrey couldn't help thinking that it would be lovelier with someone to share it with.

She stopped outside the café of her friend, G. *Friend.* Maybe he was more than that. They'd gone on dates, but because he was so friendly to everyone, and maybe because of the culture difference, she never was sure of his intentions.

Maybe, she thought, *now that things with Mason have petered out, I should go in and find out. . .*

CHAPTER TWO

Audrey scooped some spackle onto a spackling knife and smoothed it onto a divot in the stone wall in her massive living room. Smoothing it down, she got it nice and level with the rest of the wall. A little paint, and no one would ever know it was there.

She'd taped a picture of what she *wanted* the room to look like on the wall, for inspiration. She'd been studying magazines and had really wanted to go with the classic, Sicilian Baroque style. Gilded crown molding, colorful tile floors, a frescoed ceiling, mirrors on the walls, and of course, she'd have to restore the massive and opulent chandelier hanging from the ceiling. That alone would be a chore.

Then she sat back and looked over the rest of the walls in the room. *One hole down, five thousand more to go.*

The walls were atrocious. She'd thought ripping the wallpaper off would be half the battle, but once she saw what waited for her in the room, she realized she was wrong. The walls were in terrible condition; someone had just covered them with ugly flowered wallpaper to conceal that fact. It was almost as if some rabid animal had taken bites out of the walls.

Just another wonderful surprise that came with her one-dollar Mussomeli house. She was making progress, albeit slow. The kitchen was just about done. The downstairs bathroom. She'd even planted a little garden out back, in the lovely space with sweeping views of the grassy, golden Sicilian hillside. She'd finally patched that massive hole in the floor of the bedroom upstairs, but much of the upstairs and this large living room were still very much works-in-progress.

"One thing at a time is all we can do," she said, repeating a line her father had told her many times. He was a general contractor, and though he'd been absent from her life since she was a preteen, his words always seemed to stick with her. Now, he was who-knew-where . . . a place called Montagnanera, maybe. She often thought about going out to seek him, but now wasn't the time, with everything she had to do.

Right now, her "one thing" was getting this wreck of a house under control.

Wearing pajama pants and a tank top, hair done up in a messy bun, she figured she had no one to impress. This whole week, she'd been like an automaton, moving from work, to home, to work, to home, taking care of business, with no time for a social life.

She didn't *want* a social life now, after the number Mason had done on her heart. That's why, when she'd stood outside G's café, she'd decided not to go in. She didn't want to be rejected by him, too. Better to forget about men and concentrate on the work at hand. There was *a lot* of that to do.

She yawned, grabbed her glass of wine, and took a sip. Meanwhile, her wild pet fox, Nick, a rescue of her own, came over, sniffing at the tub of spackle. He let out a little squeak of distaste.

"I know, you're hungry." She stood up and dusted off her jeans. "Me too. One apple, coming up."

She took the three steps down to the kitchen, cut an apple for him, and laid it in his bowl, saving one slice for herself. He eagerly scooped it up and began to nibble as she ate hers. Something delicious and fattening from *Pepe*, the market down the street, called to her, but she resisted. The reason she'd changed into pajama bottoms the second she got home was because her jeans no longer fit her right.

As she was turning to go back to her work, a bright beam of light shone through the kitchen window, momentarily blinding her. "What the . . .?"

She pulled open the front door to find an entire camera crew standing there, spotlights at full blast. Her eyes stung. There was a camera focused right on her.

"What is this?" she cried, but she had a pretty good idea.

Her American neighbor, Nessa, was about to star in her own HGTV program. This had to have something to do with that. Nessa never stopped talking about the show.

A large man in a T-shirt that didn't quite cover his giant beer belly shrugged. "Sorry, lady," he said, sounding less than apologetic. "My orders are to film the whole block."

Film the whole block . . . including me? In my pajama pants? She wiped her cheek. *And I have spackle on my face. Perfect.*

"Nessa!" she growled.

The door swung open and her California-blonde neighbor appeared, petting her cat, Snowball. She was in full makeup, her platinum blonde hair piled on her head like a debutante. As always, ready for her close-up. "What do *you* want?"

"Maybe not to be assaulted by your cameras? Aren't you supposed to get permission before filming anyone?"

She rolled her eyes. "Oh, please. There isn't a single person alive who wouldn't kill to be a part of this production. You're lucky your—*house*, if that's what you're calling it—is even going to be filmed."

Audrey frowned. "What's that supposed to mean?"

"It means that I want people to envy where I live. Which is pretty hard when it's across the street from a junkyard!"

Audrey's jaw dropped. Just because she'd left a little pile of stripped wallpaper outside on the front stoop of her place during the demolition of the living area, it was a junkyard now? Forget the fact that Nessa had had crews of people and unlimited money to renovate her place to the lovely state it was in now, and Audrey was just one person with a limited budget. Audrey's place was the largest property in town. Owned by royalty. It would be amazing. She just needed the time and the funds to get it there.

But she didn't feel like arguing. Also . . . the guy *still* had a camera pointed at her. Was the film rolling even now?

"Just . . . please. Try not to shine lights in my windows all the time. And don't film me, if you can help it?"

Nessa scoffed. "Audrey, please. They have more interesting things to film than you." She fluffed her hair and smiled as the camera swung toward her. "Namely, me."

"All right. I'll clean the garbage up. But just—"

"Whatever. Can't you see we're a little busy here? This is our first day of filming." She looked at the cameraman. "Which of my sides is the best in this light?"

Audrey slammed the door on the camera crew and turned back toward her kitchen. She touched the walls and sighed. "You're my beautiful home. You're *not* a junkyard," she whispered.

At least, it wouldn't be when she was done with it.

The money that that vet job was offering sure would help speed it along. She could even hire someone to help. Things had been moving along steadily, though slowly, but Mason not coming by lately had brought progress to a near standstill.

Mason. *Macey.*

She sat on the stairs, grabbed her glass of wine, and drained it in one gulp. Then she poured herself another.

Who was that mysterious woman? The girl was probably a model. That's exactly what she expected for a man like Mason, who was such a pretty-boy, he could be in movies himself. She looked exotic and wild and cultured and everything Audrey wasn't. She probably never tripped over her own feet or laughed so hard she snorted wine out her nose. Her name was probably Philomena. Or Ishanti. Or Tamika. She *looked* like a Tamika.

Sitting there, in the dim light of a single lamp in the kitchen, she absently petted Nick as she looked around her home.

It wasn't a junkyard. But it still needed a *lot* of work. Work she wasn't sure she could do on her own.

She grabbed her phone and typed in the name of the island: *Lipari.*

The search returned all the answers she was looking for: *Lipari is the largest of the Aeolian Islands, an archipelago in the Tyrrhenian Sea off the northern coast of Sicily, southern Italy.*

She stared at the little cluster of islands, gnawing on her lip. Then she pulled up some photographs of the place. She saw a beautiful, white-sand beach bordering a coastline of calm blue-green waters. Narrow, serpentine cobbled streets, much like those in Mussomeli, with brightly colored homes pressed together, each one with a small, wrought-iron railed balcony and pale blue shutters. Cafes and shops bustling with people. A vibrant harbor full of yachts and small fishing boats.

I'd like to see this place, she thought.

She'd been hung up on Mason all week. Ever since that day, she'd been staying awake in bed, thinking about him, her heart hurting every time she pictured his face. She kept replaying that awful last moment in her head, wanting to cry for how stupid she'd been.

And for what? She should've gone along with her first impression of him, which was that he was far too handsome to ever be interested in her. He'd done nice things for her. Taken her in when she needed it. They'd toured Agrigento together, and he'd said some sweet things. But that was all. He'd been flirtatious, but that was just teasing. He never made any promises or indication that it was anything but friendship. She'd built it up to something else in her head.

Now, she was doing herself no good, sitting around here, moping. If she wanted things to happen, she was going to have to take the bull by the horns and *make* them happen.

If she really wanted to make progress on this "junkyard" of hers, then a little shot of money was the first order of business.

She was being silly, thinking the vet center would fall apart without her over a matter of a few days. It wouldn't. Concetta was perfectly

11

capable of handling the minor check-ups and appointments, and could call her if she had problems. It was very likely that no one would even miss her.

And it would be good to put distance between herself and this place for a little while. If she was busy in Lipari, maybe she wouldn't have time to think about *him.*

Not to mention that it would be great to escape the prying eyes of the video cameras across the street.

"What do you say, Nick?" she asked her pet, still stroking his red fur. "Want to go on an adventure?"

He yawned and snuggled in close to her thigh. Right now, it looked like all he wanted to do was sleep.

She reached for her purse, pulling out the paper where she'd scribbled Matteo Gallo's name and number. She plugged it into her phone. It rang only once before a voice said, "Gallo."

"Mr. Gallo?" Audrey asked, taking a deep breath. "It's Audrey Smart. I thought about your offer. And I accept."

"Wonderful!" he said with great excitement. "That is fantastic news."

"Yes, so when do you—"

"There is an early bus leaving Mussomeli tomorrow morning! You come to Messina and take the ferry to Lipari, yes?"

Whoa, she thought, her mind racing. *That soon? I don't even know where Messina is! And what about packing! I haven't done anything! I'm sure I'm forgetting something.* "Actually, I probably need to—"

"Not many buses from Mussomeli. You don't want to miss it."

"Oh. Okay, and—"

"Give me your email address. I email you all the details."

She recited it to him. "But—"

"I meet you at the harbor when you dock, and we speak more. Safe travels, *Dottore.*"

"Okay, but—" she said, but stopped when she realized she'd said it to dead air. He'd hung up.

She looked at Nick and shrugged. "I guess we'd better pack, bub," she said to him. "We're leaving bright and early tomorrow morning for Lipari."

CHAPTER THREE

"Are you sure you're going to be okay?" Audrey said into her cell phone for the fifth time as she sat on the old bus, pulling into the seaside town of Messina, Sicily.

For the past few hours, she'd been packed like a sardine into the seventies-style motorbus. There were no seatbelts, so it bounced the passengers around like an old school bus. It smelled like exhaust and body odor, even with all the windows open. Just when she thought she could take it no longer, a cool sea breeze wafted in, and she smiled at the first sight of the sea, as well as the port city of Messina, in the distance.

"Of course!" Concetta said brightly. "It's no problem. I just called to ask you where the extra gauze is. I have it under control."

She did seem to have a handle on everything. Audrey had lingered there, earlier that morning, making lists and quizzing Concetta on every possible thing that could go wrong. She'd checked on the strays in their care and gave them all extra cuddles. She'd told Concetta her cell phone number several times. Eventually, Concetta had just had to push her out the door, with a firm, but kind, "You go on! And don't worry at all about us!"

"I know you're more than capable," Audrey said. "But if you run into any trouble—"

"I know, I know. I have your number. Where are you now?"

"I'm just getting to Messina. I'm not sure when the next ferry is, but I'll probably be in later. I'll have my cell phone on, though, so—"

"Got it! Have a safe trip!"

Audrey hung up just as the bus turned a sharp corner. The man sitting next to her, who must've been asleep, swayed with the bus, finally resting his head on her shoulder. She gently nudged him back and gazed out the window, dipping her sunglasses to get a better look. They were just above the seaside town, descending into it, and in the distance, several islands rose out of the deep green sea. She wasn't sure which was Lipari.

She snapped a photograph and sent it to her sister, Brina, in Boston, along with the caption, *My current view.*

13

Brina replied right away with *Pretty. My current view,* and a picture of Audrey's nephew, Bryon, giggling on the changing table as his mom tried to wrangle a diaper on him.

Audrey responded with, *Cute.*

She waited for Brina to ask her where she was, or what she was up to, but her big sister and best friend didn't. Whenever they texted, Brina was much less interested in the Sicilian scenery and far more captivated—some would say, obsessed—with the man she called Abs. Mason, who did have a very nice set of them, which he liked to show off as often as possible. Whenever Audrey sent Brina a photograph of him, her sister drooled and asked for more—more photos, more details, more everything. She was almost too eager to make Mason a part of the Smart family.

But since Audrey told Brina what had happened with him, she'd been mum about it. Audrey appreciated her big sister not trying to touch on her sore spots, but she would've liked some enthusiasm about the other things she had going on in her life.

She finally typed in: *I'm heading to an island off the northern coast of Sicily to help with their stray problem. How is my nephew?*

She responded with: *Good. We all miss you here! Happy though, that you're saving the world, one stray at a time.*

The bus pulled to a stop in front of the harbor. Audrey stood up, stretched her limbs from the long ride, and collected her luggage and pet carrier. When she received it, she looked through the netting at Nick. He looked miserable. She took an apple slice from her bag, slipped it between the opening, and petted his nose. "I'm sorry, baby. I know this isn't fun for you, but the bus wasn't all that comfortable for me either. Just a little longer," she whispered.

Then she went to the edge of the dock. Luckily, the ferry was just boarding for the trip to Lipari. She got a ticket and climbed aboard the small ship, sitting out in the sun at the front of the boat so she could take in the view.

As the ferry took off, she looked at a map on her phone. There were several islands in the archipelago, of which Lipari was the most populated. She scanned the area, trying to orient herself, giving names to the various islands she saw. She found Vulcano, the active volcano nearest to Sicily, then strained to see the others. In the far-off distance, she saw a little rise on the horizon that could have been some of the other ones, and mainland Italy.

"*Ciao*," an older man said, sitting next to her on the bench. She realized he was the same man who'd fallen asleep on her shoulder on the bus. He started to speak to her in Italian.

She shook her head. "Sorry, I only got about half of that. *Non parlo molto l'italiano*," she explained. *I don't speak much Italian* was one sentence she had no trouble saying, since she said it all the time.

"Ah, you speak English!" he said, clapping his hands delightedly. He was small and wiry, and carrying a fairly large crate covered in burlap, which he set down at his feet.

She nodded. "American. You live on the island?"

"Si, Lipari is my home." He smiled wide, revealing a few gaps between his teeth. "I come to Mussomeli to pick up a friend from a cousin."

"A friend?"

He leaned over and pulled back the burlap sack to reveal a small piglet, rolled in a little ball amidst a pile of hay. Audrey patted her chest. It was so small, it reminded her of little Wilbur in *Charlotte's Web*, her favorite book growing up. She'd read that book and wanted a pig desperately, and that was probably the start of her desire to become a vet. The idea of nursing a tiny runt to health had been so appealing to her.

"Oh, he's cute!"

"What do you have there?" he asked, pointing to her pet carrier.

"Oh. This is Nick. My fox," she said, turning the carrier so he could see inside.

"Ah. Very nice. You like animals?"

She laughed. "I should. I'm a veterinarian."

"Is that right?" he said, delighted. "Well, you are certainly welcome on our island. What brings you here?"

"I've actually been summoned by the council to help with a stray cat problem?"

"*Si*. We have a lot of strays. You stay long?"

She shook her head. "No. I have a practice in Mussomeli to get back to. But I'm here to help for a few days and offer suggestions to your animal control department."

He laughed. "Animal control?" He laughed even harder, clutching his round belly. "We don't have one of those. We don't even have any animal care places at all on the island. That is why we all go to the island of Sicily for that."

"Oh." Maybe the problem was even worse than she'd thought. Mussomeli had been similar, until she arrived, with stray animals everywhere. But at least the council had been trying to do something about it, prior to her arrival. "It's really bad?"

"Yes. They have done nothing so far. Nothing. Animals all over the streets. Everywhere." He leaned in and scratched his grizzled chin. "Tell me. Do you do house calls? I have twelve cats of my own."

"Oh, um . . . twelve?" She laughed. Were they that desperate? Well, yes, they had to be, if they were offering her such a sum to come out. She had a feeling she might be very busy over the next few days, and really earn her pay. But it would be worth it. "It's a little too far to travel from Mussomeli, unfortunately. But I'm happy to stop in while I'm here!"

"Wonderful!" he said, smiling big, unashamed of his many missing teeth. The ferry banked around Vulcano, and he pointed to the island just beyond it, with a little settlement at the seaside; the brightly colored homes Audrey had seen in the photographs, climbing a hillside that was scattered with thick green trees. "That is my home. You will like it."

She smiled as seagulls squawked overhead, arcing in the pale blue sky. The sun cast its rays on the waves of the calm sea, and the pebbles on the shore glistened like diamonds. Small, colorful boats lined the beaches. As she drew nearer, she noticed a small white cathedral on the jetty, children splashing in the sea, and a fisherman dozing on the dock. The balconies of the townhomes were bedecked in flowers of every hue. It was a postcard.

Her heart swelled, and she couldn't fight the tears that came to her eyes. This—traversing the deep blue waters of Tyrrhenian Sea, surrounded by charming villages under the bright sun, was what she'd come to this part of the world for. This was like one of her dreams of this place, only a thousand times more vivid. Goosebumps sprang up on her arms. "I am sure I will. I'm sure my host will have plans for me, but can you tell me what is the one sight I should see while I'm here?"

"My home?" he suggested, winking. Then he laughed. "No, I joke. I say all of Lipari is a treasure. Just enjoy it all."

He tipped an imaginary hat to her, picked up his crate, and walked toward where the boat was docking.

She stood up, picked up her pet carrier, and looked in at Nick. He seemed to be a little happier now that he was in the fresh air. It was nicer here, with a sea breeze tossing her hair and warding off the heat from the bright sun.

"Come on, bub," she said to him as she found her way toward the exit with the small crowd of fellow passengers. As she did, she retrieved a paper from her purse. It had the address of the hotel on it. True to his word, he'd emailed her details overnight.

A little thrill passed through her as she stepped onto a long, narrow dock. A small harborside café was open, the tantalizing scent of seafood catching her attention. That would be a nice place to stop. On the pier, she smiled as she walked past a child with a bucket, collecting seashells among the rocky coastline. The moment she stepped onto terra firma, she saw a handsome older man in a jacket and tie, running toward her and waving. *"Dottore! Dottore!"*

CHAPTER FOUR

Out of breath, he grabbed her hand. "Dottore Smart?"

"Yes?"

Smiling from ear to ear, he held her hand in both of his and shook it. "Delighted! I am Matteo Gallo. I spoke to you on the phone!"

"Mr. Gallo!" she said, a little confused. He'd said he would meet her here, but she hadn't told him which ferry she'd be on. "It's a pleasure to meet you. Thank you for coming here, but . . . have you been waiting here long?"

"All day, actually. The ferry from Messina is not always on schedule, and I did not want to have you wait. You see, we're excited to have you," he said, still shaking her hand, so hard she thought he might dislocate it. "I did not want to miss you. I will help get you settled. Perhaps I can interest you in a late lunch? You must've had a long trip?"

She nodded, looking over at the café. Her mouth was watering. "Very long. I left Mussomeli early this morning."

"I trust it wasn't too bad?"

"No. It was fin—"

"Anything we can do to make you more comfortable, you just ask! I have you put up in the best hotel on the island!"

"Oh, that's all right, I'm just—"

"Yes, yes, come along," he said, grabbing her bag. He tried to take the carrier with Nick, but Nick let out an ear-piercing screech, causing many in proximity to turn. He looked at it. "Your . . . pet . . . is friendly?"

She nodded as she picked up her carrier and shushed him. "He's a fox."

He gave her an apologetic look. "The hotel might—"

"That's okay, he likes to roam outside. He doesn't like being cooped up in one place," she said, proud of herself for finally being the one to speak over him.

"All right, great," he said, ushering her off the pier. They walked down the stone harbor area, past shops selling wares for tourists, a little boy selling pumice on a corner, and to the first car, parked on the

18

corner. "I'll take you right there so you can get settled. It's not far, but after the day you've had, I'm sure you'd like to freshen up as soon as possible."

He moved quickly, getting her bag into the back and helping her into the front of the car. As she sat in the front with Nick on her lap, she got the distinct feeling that he was in a hurry. That feeling only intensified when he jumped into the car and began to tear off, away from the harbor.

I hope this is okay, she started to worry as she looked down at Nick. *I didn't even ask him for identification. What if he's some crazy man pretending to be the councilman, who just kidnapped me?*

She relaxed a bit, though, when he pointed a place out to her. "That place is my uncle's. We must go there for dinner and grappa. The best *pasta alla Strombolana* you'll ever have."

"Sounds great," she said, even though she had no idea what that was.

"And over there is the cathedral. Very beautiful. Of course you will want to see that," he said. "The town itself is very walkable, very nice. Perhaps you tour the pumice quarry?"

"Pumice, is that a—"

"Yes, that's our main export," he said. "And of course, we have the best seafood around. You will gain a little weight while you're here, eh?"

That was the last thing Audrey wanted to do, but she smiled. He'd rolled down the window, so as they navigated the tight, curving roads, she got a good taste of the charming village. She didn't notice much of a stray problem until she happened to peer down a narrow alley and saw a collection of cats congregating near a trash can. Then a black cat dashed in front of the car. There were a few sunning themselves on the front stoops of buildings. They may have belonged to someone, but they didn't appear to have collars.

"Hmm, I see the problem with strays," she said.

"Yes. It's bad here, but it is even worse near the restaurants. Some owners report that there are thirty or forty cats outside their back doors at any given time. And that number is only growing."

She gasped. "That's terrible. But Mussomeli had a similar problem. Maybe not as big, but it's getting better," she said proudly. "I think my plan had a lot to do with it getting on the right track, and I'm happy to share everything I learned with you."

"Does your plan involve . . . euthanasia?" he asked.

19

"Oh, certainly not!" she said, shaking her head. "I don't believe in that unless an animal's suffering or at the end of its lifespan. It's not these animals' faults that they were born, and most of them are perfectly happy to live on the street. But obviously to curb the nuisance, we need to cut down the number of births."

"And how do you propose we do that?"

"In Mussomeli, we've been capturing the males, neutering them, and releasing them out into the wild, or putting them up for adoption. We've been incentivizing pet owners to come in and have their animals spayed or neutered. It's actually making a difference already. It's only been in place a couple months and already the stray pet population has gone down around town."

"Is that so?" He smiled. "Well, Dottore Smart, you are a welcome addition to our island, for sure. Others have made suggestions, but I must say, that is the best plan I've heard in a long while. I'm sure the mayor will agree."

"Tell me," she said, as Nick jostled in the carrier on her lap, trying to take in all the sights along with her, "who else has been making suggestions? I met a man on the ferry who said that the animals on Lipari were having no help at all. Surely, you have veterinarians here?"

He nodded. "We do, yes. We have one other veterinarian. But—" He paused as his car came to a stop at a corner. "We're right near the largest shelter in town. I thought we could take a quick tour. Perhaps that would—"

"Yes, I'd love to see it," she said. "As soon as possible. That would give me an idea of what we're dealing with."

He checked his watch. "It's closing in another hour. You'd like to see it now?"

She nodded.

He made a sharp left and headed up a hill, out of town. "All right. Dottore Smart, I have to admit I was hoping you'd say that. You will be very welcome there."

"Great," she said. "Let's go."

CHAPTER FIVE

The sun was rapidly sinking in the sky as they arrived at the fenced-in two-story house that served as the shelter. Before she got to the front door, Audrey could already tell the place was a horror.

The small, white stucco building had its front door open, and cats seemed to have overrun the place, because they were climbing in and out of the building. There was a fenced-in area, also entirely populated by cats. Not that the fence did any good, because they seemed to be climbing the fence, coming and going as they pleased.

Matteo winced as he pulled up into a parking spot on the gravel drive. "Oh my. It does appear that the cats have overtaken it, doesn't it?"

Audrey opened the door to the car, and the second she set a foot down on the gravel, a gray cat came up to her, winding its body around her. Two more were headed her way. "Oh. Goodness," she said, carefully closing the door so as not to trap any tails.

She'd hoped to take Nick out, but at the sight, he began hissing. She decided to leave him in his carrier on the hood of the car. He'd be safe there. The last thing she needed was him getting into a catfight with a hundred stray cats.

Poor Matteo tripped over the felines several times as he made his way around the car to join her. "Right this way," he said apologetically, guiding her toward the open door.

It was like walking on a moving floor. Audrey had to squeeze to the side to accommodate all of the animals. Occasionally, she had a near-miss with a tail or a paw. The number of cat bodies of all colors and sizes only seemed to increase as she made it to the lobby. The waiting area may have once been a regular waiting room, with chairs, houseplants, and a coffee table filled with magazines, but now, every available space appeared to be covered in cats.

This wasn't like Mussomeli at all. It was *so much worse.*

"This is your largest shelter on the island?" Audrey asked, looking around. The smell of cat urine stung her eyes, and there was fecal matter everywhere. The stench was so overpowering, she could barely breathe. No wonder they'd left the doors and windows open.

21

Matteo nodded. "It is. We have a couple of smaller ones inland. But this is the one that most people bring the strays to, because of its proximity to the town itself. As you can see, it's in peril."

I'll say, Audrey thought, unable to peel her eyes off the squirming lot of cats, sitting, prancing, preening themselves. Clearly, this island was in trouble. "Do they do any spaying or neutering here?"

Matteo shrugged. "I don't know. We can ask Sabina."

"Sabina?"

"She's the manager here," he mumbled as a cat jumped from a cabinet into his arms. He quickly dropped it, looking rather green. Clearly, the stench was getting to him, too. "Oh. I think I might be sick."

He rushed out the door, cats be damned, as Audrey looked around. Were there any humans managing this place? Because right now, it wasn't looking so good. Alone, she tried to navigate toward a door in the hallway that said "Office," and finding it slow-going because of the traffic, finally called out, "Hello?"

A head popped out of one of the doors, farther down the hall. "*Si?*"

"Hi! Sabina?" She struggled with her Italian, explaining, "*Sono una veterinaria?* From Mussomeli?" and then tried to remember the Italian word for "came." "*Sono . . .um . . .*"

The woman's eyes narrowed. "Eh?"

I'm butchering my Italian. She'd probably better understand my English, even if she doesn't speak a word of it. "I came here with Matteo Gallo."

The heavyset woman came nearer, tsking at the animals as she went, wading through them confidently, as if she was used to this mess. They seemed to part like the Red Sea for her. She donned a pair of bifocals and inspected Audrey, twisting her pale, doughy face as her eyes scanned her from head to toe. "You say you're a veterinarian from America?"

Audrey nodded, relieved. Thank goodness. She spoke English.

"Not possible! What are they, hiring babies to take care of the animals in the States?" the grandmotherly woman chuckled.

Audrey paid it no mind. She'd been told the first half of her life that she was too young to do certain things, and the second half of her life, she'd been told she *looked* too young. It was her freckles. She said, "It seems you have a bit of a problem here?"

The woman laughed. "You can say that." She extended a pockmarked hand. "I'm Sabina. This is my shelter. I've run it for twenty years, and it has never been this bad. Where's Matteo? Did he get sick again? That man has no constitution whatsoever."

Audrey shook her hand. "Yes, he had to get some air. What have you been doing?"

"We take the animals in when we can, take care of them. Try to adopt them out. We have clinics to spay or neuter once a month. But it's not enough, as you can see."

Audrey bent down to look at one of the cats. It looked healthy. They all appeared healthy, without any sign of mange, though many of them seemed a bit malnourished. Of course they would be. On an island such as this, there probably wasn't enough food to go around.

"Come," she said, "let us get out of this mess."

Audrey finished with her inspection of the animals and stood up. Sabina led Audrey slowly to a room in the back of the building. It looked like a little break room, with a coffee service. Sabina tried to close the door, but one of the cats slipped through. "Out!" she cried. The cat listened, scampering away. She sighed. "It's a hard job. I supply basic medical care to the ones that are sick. Me and Vito. Coffee?"

Yes. After the early day she'd had, she could use the pick-me-up. "Sure. Vito?"

Sabina poured her a Styrofoam cup as she sat down. "My grandson. He lives with me here. So he helps me sometimes."

Audrey took the cup. When she looked inside, she saw, unmistakably, that there was cat hair floating among the steaming liquid. She immediately lost her desire. "You *live* here?"

She nodded. "Upstairs. There is an apartment. This kind of job requires a person to be on it round the clock, you see."

"It can't be very nice to be living here, though, with all the—"

"It sucks," a voice said. The door opened, and a tall, thin kid built like a basketball player with dark hair spilling in his eyes and earbuds in his ears came up behind Sabina. He hissed at one of the cats as he closed the door. Even with a pronounced, ambivalent slouch, he was almost two feet taller than her, with acne on his cheeks and a scowl on his face. "I never thought I'd say this, but it's even worse than juvie. Who are you?"

"I am a veterinarian. I've been tasked with helping the island solve its stray problem."

He snorted. "*You?* Good luck with that."

23

Ignoring the obvious barb, she tilted her head. "You don't have an accent."

"You're bright," he muttered, going to a mini-fridge. He grabbed a bottle of soda, cracked the lid, and took a long swig. "Guess that's why they gave you the doctorate."

Sabina gave her an apologetic look. "Forgive Vito. He's not had an easy time. His father is American. But there was a divorce, and he got into a lot of problems with the law back home . . . you know, stealing. Drugs. Being a boy. He's lived here with me for the past four years." She leaned in and whispered, "I've been trying to keep him in line and out of trouble."

"*Nonna*. Stop talking about me like I'm not right in the friggin' room," he muttered.

She shrugged apologetically. "But the truth is, he's not very happy here."

Obviously. And who would be, if your house was overrun by cats? As much as Audrey loved animals, *this* was too much. "Have any animals here been spayed or neutered?"

She nodded. "Some. I lose track. The vet here has been doing it, but he loses track, too."

"Matteo mentioned you have a vet here. Where is he?"

"He comes in once a month here, but even if he came in every day, it wouldn't be enough. There are so many." She rolled her eyes. "It's no good."

"So you just don't have enough cages for all the animals," she mused.

Vito laughed derisively. "Oh, we do. *Nonna* doesn't think it's humane to keep them locked up." He rolled his eyes.

Audrey's eyes widened. "What?"

She shrugged. "I know it seems strange, but I just don't think animals are meant to be in cages all the time. So I let them go in and out as they please. But at night, they have a place to stay . . ."

"Okay," Audrey said, hardly able to believe she was hearing this. She didn't like putting them in cages either, but some things were necessary to control the population and prevent them from hurting themselves. Her head ached, probably from the stuffiness inside. She closed her eyes and started to massage her temples. "You leave the cages open? All the time? Like it's a hotel or something?"

She nodded. "Yes. The animals love it. That is why they keep coming back to me! I treat them with so much kindness, and they give it back to me."

"Sabina," Audrey said gently. "It might seem humane, but it's actually not, because it's increasing the stray animal population on this island. That's why many of these animals are malnourished and not getting enough to eat. If you keep them in cages, letting them out only sporadically, it will help tremendously. They actually like having a place of their own to sleep and stay safe. Then you can keep track of them and which ones are spayed and neutered and sick. You understand that, right?"

"Well . . . I suppose. But in twenty years, I've never done such a thing. Cages are cruel."

Vito groaned. "Nonna. It's like I've been telling you. Listen to this lady. She's right."

Audrey smiled at him gratefully, but he didn't make eye contact. With that big mop of hair, she wasn't even sure the kid *had* eyes.

The woman drummed her hands on the table, thinking. As she did, Audrey looked over and noticed a ring of cat feces on the table, right near her elbow. Now she felt sick.

"Well, if you say so . . ." the woman said, her voice leaking doubt. "What do you suggest we do?"

Audrey rubbed her hands together. "First, I'd like to get the animals into their cages. Then we'll go through each one and give them an exam, to see what we're dealing with. Sound good?"

Vito nodded, finally seeming interested. "Hell yes. I'll help. Anything we can do to get these animals out of my hair, once and for all."

"Great." Audrey took the hair tie from around her wrist and put her hair in a ponytail. Then she clapped her hands. "Let's go. We have some work to do."

CHAPTER SIX

In the yard, Audrey navigated around little packages of cat poop as she tried to find the last few remaining cats. She'd seen one heading out this way—a young calico with green eyes. "Come on, Patches. Here, Patches!" she called, stooping to look underneath an old picnic table.

No Patches.

She took a deep breath and looked around. Here, on the hill behind the shelter, there was hardly any breeze. And even though the sun was fading, it was still scorching. Just beyond a line of cypress and olive trees, she could make out the sea in the distance. She hoped it would give her cooling vibes, but it didn't. It had to be well over eighty degrees even in the shade, but there was very little of that in the yard.

Very little shade, and a *lot* of poop packages. It was a big minefield.

Vito came by, holding a white cat with a spot on its tail. "I got Dot," he said, with a sheepish smile, which he quickly erased. He clearly didn't want anyone getting the impression he was enjoying himself. Gradually, he'd started talking to her, first telling her where to find different animals, and later, pumping his fist whenever he nabbed one. He didn't complain, even though he had scratches on his hands and arms.

"Good job!" she said, patting him on the back. "Put him in the last cage on the top right and I'll be in there in a second."

"On it," he said, heading inside. He was sweaty, too, his face red, but he had been a huge help. He'd been a normal moody teenager, at first, and Audrey had worried he'd constantly be giving her attitude. But he was coming around. He obviously wanted to fix this runaway cat problem just as much as Audrey did.

The shelter was getting better, too. For cats, and for humans.

A little bit of clean-up, and the yard could actually be someplace people could go, too. There was a barbecue and a picnic table there, but both were covered in excrement and looked as if they hadn't been used in ages.

Poor kid, she thought as she walked through the yard. *I can't imagine living in a place like this. I wonder where his parents are.*

Suddenly, out across the fenced yard, Nick hissed. She'd let him out when they first started rounding up the animals, because he'd always proven to be a big help in doing that. He was like a regular sheep dog when it came to getting cats to fall in line. She credited her trusty pet fox in herding most of them; he'd been a lifesaver on more than one occasion before.

She looked over and found him standing, frozen, his ears perked up as his gaze narrowed on a spot between a couple of large bushes.

Sure enough, when she stooped, she could see Patches' little white paws. The cat mewled in fright. Audrey got on her knees and reached a hand out to him. "Here, kitty kitty," she said. When that didn't work, she grabbed a handful of dry cat food and held it out.

Gradually, the kitty came out, sniffing, and came close to the food. Audrey let him nibble it a little before scooping him into her arms.

Breathing hard, she looked around, and happily found that there wasn't another cat in sight. Sure, there were more out there, probably a *lot* more, but it was a start.

Done, she thought, wiping the sweat from her brow. In fact, it was so hot today, that even though the sun was now setting, her clothes were drenched with perspiration.

As she was walking across the yard to place the last cat in its cage, Matteo came over and smiled at her. He'd been strangely absent the entire time, and looked as though he'd been spending time in air conditioning—his jacket was unrumpled and there were no sweat stains on his shirt. He held up a bottle of water. "Thought you'd be thirsty so I got you some refreshment!"

She nodded. "Thanks. I'll take you up on that. Let me just take care of this fellow."

He looked around. "Looking much better already!"

"I know. We just put the animals in their cages," she said, leaning in to whisper, "I think Sabina might be a bit of a cat lady. They have an aversion to keeping animals in cages and would rather let them have the run of the place. Unfortunately, that leads to unsafe conditions for both the humans and the animals. But I think she understands now."

Audrey went inside, and as she expected, Matteo didn't follow. Her phone buzzed. She fished it out of her pocket and found a text from Concetta. *Locking up now! Everything went great.*

Hmm. Audrey had hoped for more of an update than that. She'd had two check-ups, both routine, but she thought for sure that Concetta would have questions about them. Plus, it was barely five-thirty.

Audrey never locked up before seven, because there was always something to do. Was Concetta really more efficient than she was?

Stop worrying about it, Audrey. She's got it under control. Everything is fine.

Inside, the cool air was welcome. Though the building itself had a large room equipped with almost one hundred cages, it still wasn't enough for all the animals. They'd had to double them up. It was definitely crowded. She put Patches into the last cage, let out a sigh of relief, and wiped her brow as she closed the door. "We did it! I think I want to celebrate!"

Vito pumped his fist. "Yes!"

"You poor thing. It must've been terrible for you," she said to him. He did look like he'd just been through a war, with all those cat scratches on him. She motioned him over and got out the first aid kit, and went to work on applying antiseptic to the wounds.

He snorted. "Yeah. I'll say. There were cats everywhere. I kept telling her she needed to do this, but she wouldn't let me. They were everywhere. Even upstairs. Pissing and pooping all over the place. Every time I ate, there was cat hair in the food. It was gross."

"Where are your parents?"

He shrugged. "My father's kind of a jerk. I don't get along with him. And my mom travels a lot. She's an actress. They met in Hollywood."

"Really?"

"Yeah. They're pretty self-obsessed. So believe it or not, as bad as the cats are, they're better than my parents."

"I'm sorry."

He shrugged. "Don't be. Besides the cats, Nonna mostly leaves me alone. And this thing, with the cats . . . if it keeps going? I think you'll have made my life one hundred percent better."

Audrey smiled at him sadly. "What are the chances your grandmother will keep them in their cages?"

"I don't know." He ran his hands though his hair, and for the first time, Audrey could see his eyes. They were bright blue. "But I'm going to try to get her to. When I'm not at school. Thanks, Doctor."

"It's my pleasure," she said, looking around at the many cages. "But the work here has only begun. We need to look the animals over, see which ones can be neutered, and make sure they're all healthy."

"I'll help you," he said, almost too readily. He was such a changed kid, she couldn't help but like him.

"That would be amazing, Vito. Thank you," she said, smiling. "And here, when I first met you, I thought you didn't care very much about the animals."

"No, actually, that was why I wanted to live here, at first. I wanted to be a vet. I like cats. But not this many of them," he said as she finished applying a bandage to one of his scratches. "I don't know. Seeing you, and how much you care . . . it's kind of cool. Most people in the world don't care."

"Oh?" She wondered if he was talking about his parents. There seemed to be no love lost there.

"Yeah. Some people on this island don't give a crap at all about these animals, and would just rather see them die."

"Really?" So he wasn't talking about his parents. *That's an awfully negative view to have. I wonder where he got that from.* "Who?"

"Some people who come around here. Sometimes I think that if they could drop a bomb on this place and obliterate it, they would." He shrugged.

"Your grandmother isn't like that."

"No. She's not. She's on the opposite end of the spectrum. She cares too much. The cats drove me crazy, but I didn't want them to die," he said, swallowing. "That just seems too cruel."

"I agree," she said, snapping the lid on the first aid kit. "You're all set. There's more work to be done. But Rome wasn't built in a day. Now, what do you say we go find your grandmother and show her all the progress we've made?"

CHAPTER SEVEN

"Oh, my," Sabina said as she toured the shelter, stepping through as if she'd never been there before. Wringing her hands, her brow furrowed, she looked more concerned than delighted. "And you're sure that they're quite happy, caged up like this?"

"Quite sure," Audrey said, smiling at Vito.

The door opened, and Matteo appeared. His nose twitched from the stagnant air. He handed her the water, blinking at the tears in his eyes. She unscrewed the cap and took a long, satisfying gulp.

"It's a little late," Matteo said, looking around. "And I have to get back to the family. But this place looks great. Thank you, Dottore."

"Well, I really should do the check-ups, and—"

"Can't it wait until tomorrow?"

"It shouldn't. But I guess if there's no other choice. Thank you," she said to Sabina and Vito, looking around for her things. She grabbed her pet carrier and motioned for Nick to jump inside. Of course, he hesitated. "Come on, Nick. I'll be back tomorrow to give them check-ups."

Sabina clapped her hands. "If you really want to do the check-ups tonight, Vito can drive you back to town afterwards. That's no problem. But the least we can do for you is give you dinner right now." She nudged her grandson. "Right, Vito?"

Audrey's face fell. After the stories she'd heard, and the coffee . . .

Vito groaned. "Nonna, I don't think she likes food with cat hair in it."

"Oh, you, *mascalzone*," she said affectionately, reaching up to ruffle his hair. She couldn't quite reach, so she only managed to get the side of his head. "I meant, please, Dottore, let us treat you to dinner at a local place downtown. *Pietro's*. You will like it very much."

Audrey smiled. "I would like that."

Matteo nodded. "Yes. Great place. The best. It is the one I showed you when we arrived, my uncle's. And only a short walk from your hotel. And you can have some of the *pasta alla Strombolana* I was telling you about. You'll never have anything better anywhere, I promise!"

Sabina nodded. "That dish is great. I agree."

Audrey made a mental note of the name of the dish, even though she had no idea what it was. "I'll—" She paused when she saw Vito elusively sticking his finger down his throat, miming gagging. "I'll think about it. Shall we go?"

Vito nodded. "I'll drive."

*

The ride to the restaurant was mostly downhill, and Vito had a heavy foot. By the time they were on level ground, near the harbor, the lone bottle of water that had been swirling in Audrey's stomach had threatened to come back up numerous times. When he finally pulled to the curb and braked, Audrey lurched forward, thankful for seatbelts.

Vito cut the engine and checked the dash. "Think that's a new record, huh, Nonna?"

Sabina smiled and said to Audrey, "He dreams of competing in those car races. Vroom-vroom."

Audrey peeled her fingers off the armrest. She wished they'd told her that before she got in the car with him. "Well, I think you're well on your way," she said.

Audrey stepped out. The second she did, she noticed a cat scampering down a dark, narrow alley with a soft *meow*. Turning, she saw another sitting on the sidewalk, looking ready to pounce at something, probably a mouse.

They're everywhere, she thought.

The restaurant, Pietro's, was a small building, right on the corner. There was a small area on the sidewalk with bistro tables, and patrons were sitting out, enjoying the warm night, as the sun set over the harbor. Little candles glowed at each table. The smell of roasted garlic and olive oil was heavy in the air. It was adorable, yet another part of the dream she'd had before moving to this part of the world. Even Mussomeli had nothing so romantic.

She smiled as they stepped up to the host's stand, and her stomach growled audibly. She clutched it as Vito laughed, and explained, "I'm starving."

Sabina patted her hand as the host seated the three of them at an outdoor table. "You came to the right place for that! A bottle of your house red, Giuseppe!"

The host nodded and headed away. Audrey sat down, inhaling the bracing, briny sea air, and opened the menu. Sure enough, the special of the day was *pasta alla Strombolana*. Possibly the special of *every* day, considering the menu looked well-worn. "What does this pasta have?"

"Oh, all good stuff. Spaghetti. Olives. Tomatoes. Sea urchins," Sabina said, spreading her napkin on her lap. "You will like it."

"Sea urchins?" That was something she'd definitely never had before. But she decided to risk it. Closing her menu, she said, "So how did you come to be owning a shelter?"

"Oh." She patted her chest. "I live in that house up on the hill all my life. Just me and my Orlando, my husband. And Rosa, my daughter, Vito's mother. She move away many years ago, and then it was just us two. Empty nest. Orlando bought me a cat. I call her Pepe. I loved her more than anything. And when my Orlando passed on, I decided to get more cats. After a while, I decided I wanted even more. And then I see all the cats on the island, needing help. I start taking them in. Turned his workshop into a kennel. Now I do what I love, every day."

"Yes, but it must be exhausting, with so many of them."

She nodded. "It is," she admitted. "I think your way of organizing will help. I just . . . suppose I was afraid to do it. But you're the veterinarian. You know your stuff."

The waiter, who was just setting a glass in front of each of them, said, suddenly, "Who? *Veterinaria?*"

Sabina said, "*Si. Dottore Smart* is visiting us from America."

He'd been about to pop the cork on the wine, but he stopped and gaped at her. "Oh!" He started to speak in Italian, so fast that Audrey couldn't even translate a single word.

Sabina leaned in. "He says he has a puppy that is sick and is hoping that you can come and visit him while you are here?"

"Oh? What is wrong?"

Sabina translated for the man, and relayed his response to her. "He seems to think it might be something bad, maybe a rash, because he doesn't eat or drink very much. And his hair is falling out."

She smiled up at him. "Yes. Yes, of course. Just let me know your address, and I'll stop by as soon as I can? Perhaps tomorrow."

Once again, Sabina translated. The man nodded and smiled brightly. *"Si, si! Grazie!"* and rushed away without pouring their wine.

Sabina took over, pouring a glass for herself and for Audrey, a half-glass for Vito. Vito took a single gulp and finished the whole glass. He said, "I told you, you're going to be famous if you hang around here for long."

She took a sip of her own wine and grabbed a slice of warm bread from the table. Taking a bite, she said, "I don't understand. Isn't there a veterinarian on the island that people can take their pets to? I thought you said there was?"

Sabina nodded. "Oh, there is. Dottore Luciano Mauro." She looked over at Vito, who was shaking his head and grimacing. "He's—how shall I say this? A—"

"An idiot," Vito filled in, the smile on his face indicating he was only too happy to contribute the fact.

In shock, Sabina nudged him. "That's not nice!"

"It's true," he grumbled. "It's a wonder we have a stray problem here, considering he's probably killed half the pet population with his bad advice."

Sabina leaned in and patted his hand. "Vito. Pepe was just old. She was seventeen!"

Vito gave her a doubtful look. "Pepe was *fine*. She could've lived another couple of years at least. And he insisted on putting her down." He snapped his fingers. "Like *that*."

Sabina sighed and turned to Audrey. "Poor thing. Pepe was his first true friend when he moved here. Vito had a hard time adjusting. They went through a lot together. After Dottore Mauro got through with Pepe, Vito has never trusted the man."

"Still don't," he mumbled, grabbing for the bottle of wine. Sabina started to put a hand on his, to stop him, but then shrugged and let him pour himself a full glass.

The waiter came back and asked for their orders. Audrey said, *"Pasta alla Strombolana."*

Vito mumbled, "Your funeral," and then looked up at the waiter. "Spaghetti."

Audrey looked over at him and whispered, "What's wrong with what I ordered?"

He shrugged. "They sucker everyone into trying it when they first come on the island. It's super salty and weird. I had it when I was eleven and I still have nightmares."

She laughed. "Well, I'm here in Italy to try new things. So I guess I'll just try to stomach it." When the waiter finished taking Sabina's order and left, Audrey said to both of them, "I'm sorry this vet is such a problem. That's a shame."

Sabina nodded. "He's not quite the horror show Vito is making him out to be, but I'll admit he does not have the best reputation. There are cases of him misdiagnosing pets, treating them badly. His bedside manner leaves a lot to be desired, and—"

"Not to mention his clinic is a craphole," Vito added bluntly.

Audrey swung her gaze to Vito. "It is? Where is it?"

"Oh, yeah. It makes our shelter look like a royal palace. It's down the street. You should take a look at it," he said, taking a piece of bread and dipping it in the oil with balsamic vinegar and rosemary. "But not on a full stomach because you'll probably want to retch."

Audrey looked at Sabina. "Well, that's awful. I'm sorry."

"That's not all," she said, shaking her head.

"There's more?"

"Let's just say that there are certain rumors about him."

"Rumors?" Audrey leaned forward, intrigued. Whatever it was, it was clearly even worse than the other things they'd just spoken of. What rumors could be worse than him misdiagnosing and maltreating animals? Audrey couldn't imagine.

"Yes. I'll leave it at that," Sabina said, giving Vito eye-daggers that were impossible to miss. She'd also gone to kick him under the table. The only reason Audrey knew that was because she'd kicked *Audrey* instead. Wincing, she looked at the blunt teenager, hoping he'd say what his grandmother was clearly too polite to say.

But he didn't. Instead, he simply raised his eyebrows mysteriously and smirked.

Before she could ask him what that meant, the food came. She looked down at her dish—thick coils of homemade pasta, bits of olives and tomatoes, all in a creamy sauce. It looked and smelled heavenly.

She eagerly dipped her fork in, picked up one of the white, viscous things, and took a deep breath. It was salty, and a little sweet, like the sea. A bit like oysters. She tried another, with a bit of the pasta, and it practically melted in her mouth. She let out a little involuntary "Mmm."

"I thought you said this was terrible," she whispered to Vito. "It's delicious!"

He laughed. "You don't let anyone tell you anything, do you? That's good. You'll probably need it here, with the doctor. Because *he's* like that, too. Stubborn."

She leaned in. "What are these terrible rumors about him?" she whispered to him.

He glanced at Sabina, then back at her, then made like he was zipping his lips. "Don't worry. I'm sure someone like you will be able to find out eventually." His grin widened. "Because I can already tell. You and he are *not* going to get along."

Audrey blinked. Was he really that bad? She wasn't sure she wanted to find out, but she had a feeling that eventually, whether she wanted to or not, she was going to.

They finished their meals, and, relaxed and rejuvenated, Audrey clapped her hands. "I think we have a lot of work to do," she said, finishing her wine. "What do you say we get back to it?"

CHAPTER EIGHT

"Ouch!" Audrey shouted as a particularly feral black cat scratched her palm. She stared at the blood running down her hand, and yawned.

Then she went to the sink and ran the injury under the faucet. Covering it in a paper towel, she let Sabina bandage it as she looked around at all the faces of the animals, peeking out from the cages.

One hundred and seventy-six cats.

That's how many cats were at Sabina's shelter. Audrey and Sabina had completed the count shortly after eight PM that evening, and that was the latest tally. Then she'd set to giving each one a thorough check-up, determining any treatment needed, and making sure it had its necessary medicine. Vito assisted, while Sabina went through the shelter, cleaning up as much as possible.

At least she had a nice, full stomach.

By nine, they were all dragging, but Sabina was the worst. Vito said, "Nonna. You're tired."

"I'm fine!" the fiery old woman said, waving him away. "I have so much to do."

"Oh, you've done so much," Audrey said. "You should go rest."

"Yeah, Nonna. Go up to bed. I'll finish up here with Dr. Smart," Vito said. "We won't be much longer."

Audrey smiled at him. "Please. Just call me Audrey. Both of you."

Sabina came over to her and gave her a big hug. "You are so wonderful. We are so happy to have you here. I know I have said it so many times," she said, cupping her face in her hands, "but I want you to know how much we appreciate you."

"Thank you. But I'm happy to help. This is what I love to do."

Sabina shuffled off to her apartment upstairs, and Audrey yawned and turned her attention to tackling the tenth cat of the night. It was going to be a long slog, for sure. Coffee would've helped, but she couldn't get the thought of that cat-hair coffee out of her mind, so she stifled her next yawn and set to it.

She weighed it, then cradled the wriggling little cat on the examination table, checking its eyes and ears, feeling for any internal injuries, making sure its mouth and paws were healthy and unblemished. All looked normal.

"This one's fine," she said, handing the gray one back to Vito.

He lifted him up and stared into his eyes. "He's cute. I'm gonna call him Spike." He put him in his cage and started to fill out an information card for him.

"Sounds good," Audrey murmured, already reaching for the next one, a tan, older female who'd definitely had a litter or two before. She wondered how many cats in this shelter were hers as she set her on the scale to get her weight. Marking it down in her log book, she said, "So when was the last time this other vet, this Dr. Mauro, was up here?"

"A month ago."

"Really? And he never suggested that Sabina cage the animals?"

He laughed bitterly. "Making a suggestion like that would imply that he cares. And he doesn't." He shook his head. "He neutered a couple of animals and then billed her a crazy amount of money for it. He's worthless. But he thinks he's hot stuff."

"Really?"

"Yeah. He's a big blowhard."

Vito's face was twisted in distaste. Audrey could almost feel his hate for the man, radiating off of him. No wonder he'd been so negative when she first met him. "I'm sorry he's been so terrible to you and your grandmother."

He shrugged. "I can deal with him. My grandmother can't, though. She's too nice. And he took advantage of that. He needs to take a long walk off a short pier, if you ask me." He paused, and the next time he spoke, he was quieter. "That's why I'm glad you're here. We all are. I wish you could be here permanently."

She smiled. "I'm sorry. I wish I could." She looked around. "I guess I'd better call it a night and get to my hotel. Can you take me?"

"Which hotel?"

"The Hotel Lipari."

He nodded and grabbed his keys. "Whenever you're ready."

They walked together out to his car, and she sat in the passenger seat and braced herself for the wild ride. As they drove, she thought about what Vito had said. She hated leaving any animals in need. It was a shame that this vet didn't feel the same way. "I know I can't stay here permanently," she said to Vito. "But maybe I could give your vet some pointers?"

37

He snorted as he took a downhill bump so fast that they caught air, and bounced so hard the top of her head grazed the roof of the car. "Like he'd take them. I don't think he'd listen to anyone. Especially someone younger than him."

She gripped the armrest for dear life. "You never know. I can try. He might just surprise you, like that dinner tonight surprised me. I thought it was going to be awful."

He shook his head. "Trust me. Dr. Mauro is awful. The only way he'd change is if he was dead."

*

Audrey climbed the stairs to her hotel room in the Hotel Lipari on aching feet. When she opened the door, her first instinct was to collapse on the bed and never wake up.

But she was covered in cat hair, and she knew she'd probably have a hard time falling asleep once she got into bed. She always had trouble on a new bed, in a strange place. The room was small but well-appointed, and had an enormous claw-foot tub. She planned to make good use of that. She walked through the room and smiled. Very charming.

Yawning, she went to the window and threw back the drapes. There was a gorgeous view of the harbor, the dimly lit pier, and the sea glimmering in the moonlight. In the far distance, the twinkling lights of the town of Messina pressed against the hulking silhouette of Mt. Etna.

She found the crank on the window and opened it, taking in the cool sea air, letting it fill her lungs. Nowhere in America could she see anything so beautiful. She stood there, listening to the waves lapping at the shore, and decided that yes. Even with all the trials she'd had, coming all this way from Boston had been worth it, even just for a sight like this.

Then she kicked off her shoes, went to the bathroom, and ran herself a nice bath.

As the water filled the giant tub, she checked her texts. Nothing from Concetta. She had one from Brina, a picture of her young nieces snuggling together on a couch. She wished she could be there to give them a hug.

That was one thing she missed most of all . . . family. Mason had at least gotten his mom to visit. And . . . his girlfriend? But no one had visited Audrey yet. Having no family at all in this hemisphere made her feel lonelier.

Well, she did have one person . . . maybe . . .

She stripped off her clothes and slid into the warm water, thinking of her father. He was a general contractor in Boston. She'd been his right-hand woman right up until her early teens, always accompanying to his renovations of Back Bay mansions.

Then, suddenly, he was gone. No phone calls, no letters, nothing. It was like he'd vanished into thin air. No, it was even more than that. Her mother never spoke of him. It was as if he had never existed at all.

But from her dreams, she'd had an inkling of where she might find him, if ever she got up the nerve to look.

Montagnanera. It meant Black Mountains. He'd kept a postcard of it, and had wanted to travel there one day. It wasn't far away, in the north of Italy, on the Mediterranean Sea. She'd seen pictures of it, with whimsical, brightly colored buildings in the warm sun, cobblestone streets, quaint cafes.

She'd never been this close to that place. She could go there, one day. Soon.

But her life was busy. There was so much to do, here and in Mussomeli.

Of course, that was just an excuse. Really, she was afraid of what she might find. Or what she might *not* find. What if he didn't want to see her? What if when he left her, all those years ago, it was on purpose, because he didn't want to talk to her ever again?

She dunked her head, took the sweet-smelling shampoo from the corner of the tub, and lathered up her hair. As she did, she forced herself from thoughts of her father and concentrated on her to-do list for the following day:

Morning house call to the sick puppy of the waiter at Pietro's.
Visiting the shelter and giving check-ups to the remaining animals.
Neutering any males that have been caught.
Catching additional stray males to neuter.

Yes, it would be a long day. Not only that, but she'd have to meet up with the other veterinarian, eventually, to see how she could help him.

As she washed the suds from her hair, she thought about what Vito had said about Dr. Mauro. Was he really that bad, or was Vito just teasing her, like he'd done with the pasta? She had to wonder. *Trust me. Dr. Mauro is awful. The only way he'd change is if he was dead.*

When she opened her eyes, Nick was sitting on the edge of the tub, looking at her curiously. "So, what do you think, bub?" she asked him. "Do you think Dr. Mauro is as bad as they say?"

He merely looked at the soapy water with a hint of disgust. She flicked a little water at him, and he scampered off, yelping. She climbed out of bed and sighed when she saw the time on her phone. It was almost midnight. "I think we'd better get to bed."

She had a feeling that tomorrow, she'd have her work cut out for her.

CHAPTER NINE

The following morning, Audrey set out bright and early. The GPS on her phone told her that the waiter's apartment was only a couple of blocks from the Hotel Lipari, so she walked outside, enjoying the cool morning air. Seagulls squawked above and locals called *Buongiorno* to her as she walked. Nick stayed close by, weaving in and out of the many bicycles parked on the sidewalk. Occasionally, he'd stop to sniff something interesting, then quickly scamper to keep up with her.

As she was walking, a car beeped next to her. She looked over and saw Vito, leaning over from the driver's side.

"Hey," he said. "I thought you'd be up early! Nonna said to come down and see if you needed a ride to the shelter."

"I do," she said. "But first I need to pay a house call to this person. Our waiter, remember?"

"Right," he said, flipping the locks on the old car. "I'll take you. Hop in."

She winced. They'd nearly gone off a cliff the last time. She'd need a ride up to the shelter later, since that was an uphill mile, but for this, she preferred to keep her feet on the ground. "I don't think it's very far . . ."

"Suit yourself." He jerked the car into drive and screeched off.

She came to a small townhome with a peeling blue front and checked the address. *Dodici via la Rada.* "This is it. Apartment A," she said to Nick, climbing the front step.

As she did, someone came up behind her. She whirled to find Vito. He grinned.

She gave him a confused look. "You're coming with me?"

He nodded. "Marco doesn't speak English. You don't speak Italian. You need me."

"Oh." He was right. She hadn't realized he'd even spoken Italian, because everything he'd said to her so far had been in English, but it made sense that he knew the language. Yes, he could be helpful to her. "All right. Thanks. Come on."

She knocked on the door.

The waiter who had served them last night opened the door immediately. His eyes widened with delight. *"Dottore!"*

"Ciao, Marco. *Posso . . . vedere . . . il tuo . . . cane?"* she spit out with some difficulty. Marco winced, so she looked at Vito, who shrugged. "I came to check on your dog? *Cane?"*

"Grazie!" He took her hands in both of his and dragged her inside to a small, dark apartment, with dark paneled walls and seventies decor. As he brought her down the hallway, she looked around and saw crosses and religious relics all over the walls. A television played at a low volume somewhere. The hallway opened up to reveal a larger room with an overstuffed couch. Lying atop the couch was one of the biggest Mastiffs she'd ever seen.

And it was definitely no puppy.

"What's his name?" she said, dropping her first aid kit and kneeling in front of him.

Vito did the translation. "Fabio."

"What seems to be the problem with you, Fabio?" she asked the poor animal in her sweet, baby voice, lifting his paw. He gave her his sad puppy eyes as Vito did the translation.

Vito said, "He thinks it's mange."

"Mange? Who told him that?" she said, checking his skin. Sure, his fur was uneven and patchy in places, but his gums weren't healthy and his eyes were glassy. This was something completely different, the classic signs of a malnourished pup.

"Why, it's not?" Vito asked.

She shook her head. "Not at all. Not even close. What has he been eating?"

Vito translated to Marco, who responded. Marco brought out a brand of kibble that Audrey had never seen before. Whatever it was, it wasn't the good stuff. The poor pup definitely needed a new diet right away.

The dog was just not eating the right foods. She wrote this down on a pad and paper, as well as a couple of other items that she thought would help. All of the items should have been easily obtainable at any market. As Audrey finished writing the list, Marco and Vito continued to converse, Audrey only making out a few of the words.

Suddenly, Vito let out a big, "Ha! I thought so. Get this." He leaned in close to Audrey, smiling smugly. "Dr. Mauro has been treating him for months. For *mange*. And no surprise, it's not getting any better."

Audrey's mouth shaped an O. "Well, yes, that's no surprise. Normal methods for treating mange won't help this. I'm writing out a list that will give you a cocktail of vitamins that you can get at any store. That should clear this up in a period of a week or so, and keep his coat as healthy and shiny as a newborn puppy's. Okay, Marco?"

When Vito translated, Marco leaned over, grabbed her hands, and kissed them both, numerous times. As he did, he murmured in a low voice, something that sounded like a prayer.

Vito rolled his eyes. "Don't get a big head, but he said you are a lifesaver, a gift from God. I think he's asking for a blessing from the saints to give you long life and many children. Or something."

"That's . . . nice." *Can he throw a boyfriend in there, too?* Then he stopped murmuring, and the kissing began again. "Now, what is he doing?"

"No clue. I think he's just really happy."

Audrey stared at him, eyes wide, as he continued to lavish kisses on her hands, bowing in reverence. It was almost embarrassing. She attempted to tear her hands away, but that only made him hold them tighter. He murmured something else.

Vito explained, "He's asking how much you want for the house call."

Audrey shook her head. "Oh. Please. Nothing. It's my pleasure."

"Are you sure?" Vito looked doubtful.

"I'm sure." *Though it would be nice to have my hands back.*

When Vito told him the news, he kissed them more. She finally had to rip her hands away, rather savagely, smiling at him. "I'm glad you're happy. Please, let me know if there is anything else I can do."

Marco held up a finger and returned a moment later, holding a little medal of a saint on a chain. "For you," he said.

She held it up and peered at the small writing. "Saint Christopher."

He nodded. *"Si. Si."*

Vito said, "He's saying, *God be with you in your travels.*"

She smiled and slipped it over her head, letting the medal rest against her chest. She decided she needed it, if only to survive the next drive up to the shelter with Vito.

"Please, do let me know if there's anything else I can do for you and Fabio!" she said as she stepped outside with Vito on her heels.

Vito closed the door and shook his head. "Don't offer that. He might take your magnificence up on the offer to kiss your hands again, and then we'll never be able to get you two apart."

She smiled and touched the medal around her neck. "Let's go back to the shelter. And could I trouble you not to drive like you're trying to win a race?"

He smirked. "What's the fun in that?" he said, but even so, when they were in the car, he did seem to pay attention to his speed. He stopped fully at the stop signs, too, and even let a little old lady pass on the street in front of him without revving the engine or inching forward.

She started to thank him for being so careful as they made the final turn out of the downtown area, when she saw a tiny face in the bushes. It moved to the edge of the road, testing it carefully. As Audrey watched, another face appeared. And another.

Vito put his foot on the gas and upshifted. This had disaster written all over it.

"Stop!" she screamed.

CHAPTER TEN

Vito jammed on the brakes, making them both lurch forward. When he'd caught his breath, he said, "What was that all about?"

Audrey was already taking off her seatbelt. She opened the passenger-side door and scrambled out of her seat, then ran to the side of the road, which was covered with dust and gravel. Squatting low, she peered into the bushes, trying to spot the animals, but they'd run away.

Vito came to stand beside her. "You're the one who didn't want any accidents. And you almost got us into one. What's going on?"

She squinted into the shade of the bushes. "I could've sworn I saw—" Just then, something moved. She pointed. "There!"

He stooped so he was on her level. "What am I looking at?"

Slowly, she made out their forms. "There's one, two, three kittens and their mom over there, I think. Wait right here." She motioned to Nick, who'd come to the side of the road to see what she was up to. "Come on, bub. Let's go see if we can get them."

"Wait!" Vito said, reaching into the car.

"What?"

He pulled out a box of latex gloves and handed her a pair. "Last time I handled a cat from an abandoned field, I got the worst rash. Now I never leave home without them."

She snapped them on. "Thanks."

The road was on a rather steep, stony ledge. Grabbing hold of a tree branch, she slowly lowered herself down, her sneakers slipping on the gravel as she went. After a few steps, she had to let go of the branch to move forward. When she did, she found herself rushing forward, unable to stop, fueled by gravity, her legs nearly slipping out from underneath her. Nick screeched a warning, and she thought for sure she would go somersaulting part of the way.

Finally the ground evened out at another residential road, and she regained her footing in the midst of a tangle of bushes. Now she was in an overgrown lot, bordered by chain-link fence. A virtual heaven for cats, with lots of hiding places to duck into. She looked around, trying to gauge where the cats had gone. Predictably, her less-than-graceful descent had scared them all away. After meandering around the scrubby bushes and coming up empty-handed, she bent over to look under some cars that were parked at the curb in front of the lot. Nothing.

As she walked along the sidewalk, making little cat noises to coax them out of their hiding spot, some people who lived in the townhomes across the street stopped what they were doing and watched her. One man in a white undershirt, who'd gone out to get the morning newspaper, scratched his armpit and shouted, *"Cosa fai?"* at her. What are you doing?

She ignored him. *I ask myself that every day.*

Vito came sliding down the embankment, only slightly more gracefully than she'd done. He shoved his hands in his pockets and swaggered over to her. "Are you sure you're not imagining these cats?"

She glared at him. Did he really think she'd just made them up?

But then Nick screeched. She swung around to find him keeping watch over a bush. The bush was hissing slightly.

She motioned to Nick to keep the pressure on from that angle and went around the other side of the bush. Somehow, Nick seemed to know exactly what she meant. He stalked forward, his ears perked up and his fur raised at his back, as if ready to pounce. The cat hissed some more, then backed out of the bush.

Right toward where Audrey had positioned herself.

The second it turned to run, she reached forward and scooped it up. "Aha! Got you!"

The animal screeched and pawed at her. A claw sliced across the side of her chin. "Ouch!" She dropped the cat and he raced away. She touched the side of her face and found it damp with blood. *Great.*

"He got you pretty bad," Vito announced.

"She," Audrey corrected, wiping the blood from her face. It stung, but she'd had worse. "It's not too bad. I'll be fine. I told you there was a cat there. And a couple kittens. There!"

She started to run after it. Vito joined in with her. In this game of cat and mouse, they were definitely the losers. Every time they seemed to get close, the agile kittens would dodge away. They ran in circles until they were out of breath. Just when she thought she'd outsmarted them, they'd perform a bob-and-weave maneuver that left her hands empty. She couldn't even get her hands on them. Even Nick was stymied, and had gone off through the field to chase a butterfly.

When she and Vito both lunged at the same kitten at the same time and bonked heads, Audrey groaned. The man on the other side of the street, who'd sat on his front stoop to watch the commotion, was laughing so hard, his belly shook. *"Idiotas!"* he cried, as a man with his dog stopped to watch, too. On the busy sidewalk, people were stopping all over, taking the time to watch the show.

Yes. Probably, Audrey agreed. *We are idiots, wasting time doing this when we have hundreds of cats waiting for us back at the shelter.*

"Forget it," she said, rubbing the side of her head. There was a goose egg there. Then she swiped a hand down her cheek. Her blood was already crusting there, but the sting had already subsided. "These kittens are more trouble than they're worth."

Vito wiped the dirt from his hands. "I need a nap after that."

Vito was already grabbing onto a branch and climbing up the way they'd come. Audrey looked up the steep embankment, to where Vito had parked his car.

I'll probably kill myself if I try to climb up the way I came down, she thought, searching for another way. The road went uphill, switchback-fashion, which looked considerably less arduous. She pointed and called, "I'm just going to go around. I'll meet you there!"

He gave her a thumbs-up and continued on his way.

She headed for the sidewalk. Even that wasn't an easy route, because it veered sharply uphill, but it was better than scaling the side of the ledge. By the time she'd taken a few steps, she was really out of breath. As she paused, she saw it.

A little black-and-white-striped kitten, sitting on the curb, meowing miserably.

"Ha," she said, reaching down. The little kitten actually moved toward her, allowing her to scoop it up. She cradled it in her arms. "Got you, cutie. What's your name? Let me see . . . I guess Vito would probably call you Stripe."

She was so busy checking the animal over that she didn't notice anyone approaching until a shadow descended over her. She looked up to see a man in a red windbreaker rushing toward her.

*

The man was slight, balding on top, the dark hair from his combover standing straight up on the breeze. He had a benevolent smile on his face, but his cheeks were mottled with scars which gave him the appearance of toughness.

That's probably why she took a step back. "Can I help you?"

47

"You were attempting to catch that kitten? Is he yours?" the man said in perfect English, with just the slightest hint of an accent.

"No. But I'm the new vet here, and I'm trying to round up the strays," she explained, stroking Stripe between his ears. He purred contentedly. "There are quite a lot of them around."

"Oh, I know," the man said, scratching the side of his mouth, where he had only the thinnest line of a moustache. "They are a problem. You are a vet?"

She nodded and checked her phone. It was after nine now. *Oh, he's going to ask me to pay a house call to his sick pet now, too, I bet,* she thought hurriedly. *And then I'm really never going to be able to finish up with all those animals at the shelter.* "Yes! It's very busy." She moved past him on the sidewalk. "I'd love to chat but—"

"I'm a vet, too," he said, a sick smile spreading over his face. "And I'm a little concerned with something I've been hearing."

Audrey inhaled sharply. Was he . . . Dr. Mauro, the other vet on the island? The man Sabina and Vito had said was messy, egocentric, and prone to misdiagnosing pets? "Um . . . what is that?"

"Well," he said, now smoothing his moustache as he gave her a hard stare. "I've been hearing that someone else—another vet—has been seeing my patients."

Audrey's mouth opened, but nothing came out. She'd been stunned speechless.

"You wouldn't know anything about that, would you?" he asked, almost sweetly.

Her first instinct was to lie, but she knew that would get her nowhere. She lifted her chin and said, "Well, I suppose that would be me. Are you Dr. Mauro?"

He nodded. "Indeed I am."

Jostling the kitten in her arms, she stuck out her hand. "Then, wonderful. I have been meaning to meet with you. I only arrived yesterday but I am sure we have a lot to discuss."

"Do we?" He stared at her hand as if he'd never been offered one to shake before. "I don't think we do. This is my town, my island. Lipari."

She nodded, lowering her hand. "I understand that, Doctor. And it's not at all my intention to step on your toes. In fact, I have a practice in Mussomeli. I only—"

"Then I suggest you go back there."

"I was invited here by the council, to look into the stray problem."

"The council?" One of his eyebrows arched significantly higher than the other. "Who on the council asked for you? It can't be anyone of importance, because the mayor knows that I am taking care of the stray problem."

She looked around. "From what I can tell, from my short time here, the stray problem is bad, and only getting worse," she said, her tone flat. "Look, as I said. I don't mean to step on your toes. I am only here for a few days. But I thought you could use the extra manpower. And that maybe you and I could put our heads together and—"

"Nonsense!" he said, waving his hand at her to silence her. His eyes scraped over her, from head to toe. "What are you? Just a child! And an American, at that. You think you're going to tell me my business? You're out of your mind. I've been practicing veterinary medicine for more years than you've been alive, little girl."

Little girl? Audrey's brow wrinkled. "I'll have you know that I graduated from vet school almost ten years ago and was employed by one of the best clinics in Boston before—"

He snorted. "I don't care. You know nothing. If you did, you'd understand that this profession is not about where you graduate from. It's about years in the field. That's where a vet proves his worth. Not by anything else."

Audrey stood there, stunned, vaguely aware that the people who'd been watching her try to collect the strays were now watching this whole altercation. She started to argue, but he turned away.

Then he turned back quickly, wagging a finger at her. Spittle flew from his thick lips as he spoke, spraying her in the face. "You stay out of my way, little girl. If you want, stick to catching strays. You'll at least provide a source of amusement for people. But leave the real vet work to the professionals. I'm warning you."

Audrey's jaw dropped. Was that a threat? And she'd only been offering to cooperate with him, not move in on his business. She thought he'd be happy! Her mind raced, searching for a witty reply, but the only thing that came to her was the classic, uber-professional comeback: *I know you are, but what am I?*

Before she could think of something intelligent to say, he stomped off.

As he did, a young woman approached. She had a bandana on her head, corralling a mass of long, light hair, and a long skirt. She was barefoot, and carrying a small pit bull. "*Dottore,*" she said sheepishly.

"I hope you don't mind, but I overheard you talking. Could you look at my dog, please? He has something in his paw."

"Certainly," she said loudly and extra-sweetly, looking around for the crazy vet who'd threatened her. But he was already gone. "Has he been seen by Dr. Mauro?"

The woman shook her head. "Oh, no. He is not a good doctor."

Audrey bent to have a look at the animal's paw. *Apparently, neither am I.*

When she turned the paw over, she saw the problem. A thorn. Nothing too terrible. "Come with me. I have my bag in the car, just up the street," she said.

She and her newest patient went to the car, where Vito was waiting, leaning his long, lanky body up against the side of it. She handed the cat to him. "Got one, at least. This little guy is named Stripe. Let me just check on this dog and then we can be on our way."

She grabbed some tweezers from her medical bag and performed the simple operation right there on the curb. Her patient was very good, only squirming a bit as she pulled the thorn from between the pads of his paw. As she wrapped his paw in gauze to stop the slight bleeding, he licked her face.

Well, at least someone on this island appreciates me.

"All done," Audrey announced proudly.

The woman smiled and thanked her, then offered to pay her with a beaded necklace she'd been wearing. Audrey shook her head. "No charge. Please."

The woman was dumbfounded. "Are you sure?"

"Of course! It was a simple, two-minute procedure. I couldn't charge you for something like that."

She still seemed unsure. "You won't send me a bill? Because I still owe Dr. Mauro two hundred Euros for a ten-minute visit from last month."

"I'm so sorry," Audrey said, giving the pooch a pet. *And I really wish I could stay here longer. Or that your vet wasn't a money-hungry jerk.*

Vito grinned at her. "Saint Audrey. They'll erect a statue to you before your time here is up, you know."

"Oh, stop." She went around the car to get into the passenger's side, and sat down, the kitten on her lap. As she was about to close the door, Nick jumped in, hissing at the cat. He was always so possessive of

Audrey. "Sit in the back, Nick, and don't be a baby. You should know by now, you're not being replaced."

As Vito drew his long legs under the steering wheel, he said, "I told you the vet here's a piece of work."

She sighed. "I know that now. I actually just met him."

Now it was Vito's turn to look surprised. "What? When?"

"In the street."

"Oh . . . well, that makes sense. His clinic's right there." He pointed vaguely.

"Where?"

She followed his pointed finger to a tiny building with a placard on the door that said, in letters so faded, it was hard to see, *Dott. Ma o.* The U and the R were missing entirely. Not exactly great advertising; it was almost as if he didn't want anyone knowing he had an office there. The rest of the place looked just as shabby. There were a bunch of grass clippings out front that hadn't been swept up, the stones on the sidewalk were a trip-and-fall accident waiting to happen, and the orange paint on the façade was peeling to reveal the rotten wood underneath. "Hmm," she said, peering up at it. "I wish I'd known before we stopped here. Maybe I could've met him under better circumstances."

"It can't have gone good. You're all red."

She peered at her face in the side-view mirror. She was beyond that—red, sweaty, and tired. She looked as if she'd run a marathon. "He threatened me to stop intruding on his business of taking care of the animals in this town. Can you believe that?"

"Yep." He shrugged as he pulled away from the curb. "I told you. He's a scumbag."

"I thought you were exaggerating. But he really seems to have a bad reputation. Not to mention that he overcharges people like that poor woman. No wonder you guys are in trouble." She clenched her fists on her lap and frowned, hardly paying attention to Vito's near miss with a bicyclist until the tires screeched under them.

"So what are you going to do?" he asked as he overcorrected and nearly hit a trash can on the curb.

She shrugged, cradling the kitten on her lap while Nick whined in the back seat. "What I have to do. Take care of the animals. That's my job. If he doesn't like it, let him come at me."

Vito laughed as he drove around a corner, and the shelter came into view. As tired as she was, the sight energized her, because she knew

51

she could make a difference there, and now, because of her run-in with Mauro, she was really motivated to. Vito drummed his hands on the steering wheel and said, "I knew I liked you."

CHAPTER ELEVEN

"Sabina!" Audrey called as they went inside the shelter. She looked around, still cradling a squirming Stripe in her arms. "We're here! Reporting for duty!"

"Over here!" Sabina called from the kennel area.

Audrey peeked into the reception area and smiled. They'd been busy while she was gone. The place was animal-free now, and clear of cat hair and feces. Someone had even put a few magazines on the coffee table. It looked like an actual waiting room. "This is looking good!" she remarked to Vito.

He shrugged. "Well, you might be the guru of everything animals, but I know my way around a mop. So there," he teased.

She laughed and followed him into the kennel. There, she found Sabina, sitting in a rocking chair near the window, with five of the cats surrounding her. She was reading them an Italian children's story.

Audrey cast a confused look at Vito. Vito rolled his eyes and said, "They're her babies."

"I see that," she whispered, taking Stripe to an empty kennel. When she'd successfully gotten him situated, she looked around. "Okay, I'm going to continue giving the examinations. Vito, I want you to make sure you keep a list of the males that need to be neutered, because we'll be handling that next, and then releasing the animals into the wild to make room for the ones that need us. Make sense?"

Vito nodded.

They washed up at the sink, donned gloves, and started where they had left off the night before, easing into a groove, inspecting the animals one by one.

Vito was a perfect assistant, handing her the first animal of the day after checking his vitals.

Which reminds me. I haven't heard anything from Concetta today. Should I be worried?

As she examined a gray kitten, she peered in her pocket at her phone. No messages. Not even an *Everything's going well.* She handed the kitten to Vito and quickly typed to Concetta: *Just checking to make sure everything's okay?*

A moment later, the response came through: *Perfect! No problems. When will you be coming home?*

I'm not sure, she responded, as she looked over the long rows of cages. This definitely was not the two-day appointment that Matteo Gallo had hired her for. In fact, she wasn't sure she'd be able to get it all done if she had the *week*. If she was going to examine all these animals and neuter the males, she had to get a move on.

She pocketed her phone and was just about to continue her examination on the kitten when the door from the outside opened. The councilman strode in, wearing a full suit, casting a scrutinizing eye over the place. He glanced at Sabina, who didn't even pause from the story she was animatedly telling to the cats, who seemed more interested in cuddling Sabina than the story itself. His lips curled into something like disgust.

But his expression changed when he saw Audrey.

"Ah, Dottore Smart!" he said, clasping his hands together. "The woman of the hour. I was just telling the mayor about the way you'd transformed this place from a wreck to a respectable shelter. We are so—" He paused and touched his cheek. "What happened there?"

"Oh. Nothing. Just a war wound," she said, touching her own face. Crusty blood flaked off. She probably should've seen to it, but she had other things on her mind.

"Well. As I was saying. We are so proud."

"I beg your pardon, Councilman Gallo," she said as she removed the stethoscope from her ears. "But I had a lot of help with Vito and Sabina. I helped get the animals caged, but they're the ones who've been cleaning this place up. It looks good, doesn't it?"

"Incredible! My allergies are barely acting up. I don't sneeze like crazy whenever I come in here," he said, peering into one of the cages. "It's a miraculous change and it's one that we're very happy for."

"Of course. I'm happy to help," she said, almost feeling guilty. They might have been happy, but they were paying her an arm and a leg for the service. Considering most of the island was struggling to pay for basic animal care, she wondered if she should be doing more. "I still have much more to do, but I think it's coming along. I'll have the males neutered by tomorrow and released and then—"

"Would you be able to stay on another day to catch additional strays? I'd love you to talk to the council about the plan, going forward. They're very interested in hearing alternative ideas, and yours was most welcome."

"I suppose, but—"

"You'll be compensated, of course. The daily rate."

Whatever that is. She couldn't argue with that. Not with all the bills she had waiting for her at home. Plus, Concetta was fine back in Mussomeli. She wouldn't complain. "I'd love to."

"Perfect. Now . . . Do you have any other recommendations you'd like to go over with me?"

She did. Most importantly, she'd wanted to go over her findings and thoughts with Dr. Mauro. That way, she could help him make the needed changes so that he could carry the torch while she was gone. But it was clear Dr. Mauro wanted nothing to do with her. Without his help, all of her recommendations wouldn't be worth anything, and it was going to be an uphill battle to get these animals the care that they needed. It was on the tip of her tongue to say, *Find a different permanent veterinarian for the island,* but she hesitated.

"Yes," she said instead. "But why don't I put all my recommendations together and we can discuss it later? I have a lot of them, and a lot of work to do here first."

He nodded. "Oh, of course, of course. I love seeing these animals in such good hands. Mussomeli is very lucky to have you, Dottore Smart, and so are we."

He turned, startling a stray, who hissed. He backed up, then nodded at Sabina before making his exit. Audrey smiled as she watched him go.

Vito snapped, startling her out of her thoughts. "Can we keep going?"

"Oh. Sure. Yes. Where were we?"

"On number twenty-two," he said, scanning his clipboard. "Doctor, it's a wonder you don't have a big head, with everyone saying how wonderful you are all the time."

She gave him an elbow to the ribs and continued on with the examinations. It was definitely going to be a long day.

*

Audrey yawned as Vito dropped her off in front of the hotel.

It was only seven in the evening, but she was exhausted. Other than the time she'd spent at the kennel, she'd also spent a few hours after lunch alone with Nick, trying to track down more strays like Stripe.

She'd gotten four of them, and had the scratches to show for it. None of them had gone without a fight.

Now her muscles ached from the exertion. Her eyes crossed, and she couldn't see straight. All those cat chases and examinations had made her almost delirious. She was sure she'd dream about cats tonight. She almost couldn't find the door handle to let herself out. Groping aimlessly, she finally caught it and pulled.

"You going to be okay?" Vito asked.

"Of course," she yawned. "With a good night's sleep. Thanks."

"You sure you don't want to go get something to eat?" he asked, pushing aside his hair so she could see his eyes. "My treat."

"*Your* treat?" She laughed. "And how do you have the money to—"

"I do," he said, a hint of pride in his voice. "I wash dishes at Pietro's on the weekends."

"Wow. Vito. You're really busy. But save your money. You going away to school?"

He shrugged. "Not right away. I don't want to leave my grandmother alone." He tapped the side of his head. "She's not all there anymore, if you know what I mean."

"Oh," she said. Seemed like a lot of responsibility to be saddled on one eighteen-year-old boy. She wished she could do something for him. "I'll see you tomorrow? Maybe we can catch some more cats?"

He smiled. "Yeah. Sounds good."

She stepped onto the curb, Nick following close behind. She closed the door and waved. She expected him to tear off, tires screeching, but he watched until she was inside the hotel door. It was only when the door had closed behind her that she saw the red of his taillights streak across the glass. She pushed open the door and watched him leave, gnawing on her lip. *Audrey. I hope someone hasn't developed a crush on you. But that's just your luck. You finally find a man to fall head over heels for you, and he's half your age.*

Sighing, she started back inside when it hit her. She wasn't as upset about Vito maybe having feelings for her. That, she could easily deal with. What hung more heavily over her was the thought of Dr. Mauro.

What an arrogant jerk.

Then she thought about Concetta, who was only doing her job, and doing it well, and Audrey couldn't help but be a little jealous. For what? Concetta didn't even have her license yet! Envy was totally unwarranted. She had to admit that if Concetta had moved in on

Mussomeli and started caring for the animals without so much as a word to her, she'd have been upset, too.

So maybe Dr. Mauro's response to her was justified.

She hadn't been very nice to him either. She'd gotten defensive with his *Little girl* comments. They were both short-tempered at the time, and had flown off the handle. Maybe now that they'd had time to let the dust settle, they could come together and have an understanding.

It was worth a try.

As she stood there on the front stoop with Nick, she said, "What do you say we take a little walk, bub?"

He was already three steps ahead of her when she started out.

The narrow streets were only sparsely lit by streetlights, and she wasn't sure if it was safe. She didn't know exactly where she was going, but she had an idea. She turned a corner, following, based on memory, the route Vito had taken out of town, and smiled when she saw the crumbling building on the corner that belong to Dr. Mauro.

It was dark inside, so she expected he must've gone home for the night. But when she tried the door, it opened.

She looked at Nick. "Stay here, bub. I'm just going to go in and try to clear the air. I won't be long."

She went inside and found herself in a small, darkened vestibule. There were two glass doors on either side. Squinting in the moonlight cast in through the door, she read on one of them, *Dr. Mauro, Veterinaria.* Beyond it, she could see the shapes of chairs in the darkness, and what looked like the typical waiting room.

The place was clearly closed.

She pulled the handle, thinking that one, for sure, would be locked. But that one opened, too.

That's odd, she thought. Yes, the place was shabby an ill-kept, but did the man usually leave his place open when it wasn't operating?

Stepping through, she hesitated, letting her eyes adjust to the dim light being cast in from the one small window in the room. "Hello?" she called, her voice echoing hollowly through the room.

She took another step in, and another, until she almost tripped on the coffee table in the center of the room. Looking around, she could just barely see the old pictures of animals on the wall, the old, mismatched vinyl chairs bleeding their stuffing, a fish tank humming in the corner of the room. The place was hopelessly cramped and small, and smelled like cat litter. There was a door near the reception desk, but it was closed.

Turn around, a voice inside her said. *This isn't good.*

Audrey ignored it. Instead, she focused on a sound, beyond the gurgling of the aquarium's filter in the corner. It was the sound of running water and it sounded like it was coming just beyond the door. Had someone left a faucet on?

"Hello?" she called again. "Dr. Mauro?"

She took a step toward the door, miscalculating where the coffee table was, and jammed her shin against the sharp corner of it. The pain was like fireworks. She hunched over, mouth shaped in a silent scream, before clutching the sore spot and letting out a muffled, "Sugar!"

Once the pain had subsided, she carefully navigated around the rest of the furniture and made it to the door. Now, the sound of running water was even louder. The door wasn't closed; it was open, just a crack, and beyond it, she could see a slim strip of light.

She pushed it open and peered around it slowly. "Hello? Anyone here?"

The first door was dark, but open. From there, she could hear a scratching sound, and then the whimper of a small animal. She flipped on the light, her eyes slowly adjusting to a couple of kennels. Most of them were empty, but there was a single pup cowering in the middle one. He yipped when he saw her.

"Hey, sweetie," she said to him, offering him her hand to sniff. "Where's the doctor? Do you know?"

He pressed his wet muzzle against her fingertips in answer.

"I'll be right back," she said, going out to the hall again.

There was a bright light coming from the room a couple doors down. The sound of water was definitely coming from there. Audrey took a few more steps toward it, noting the fixtures similar to the ones in her own exam room—a prep table with a sink, cabinets, and an examination table. These were worn and rusty, and the instruments were scattered about with no rhyme or reason, as opposed to Audrey's method of neat arrangement. The linoleum tile was dirty and worn.

But yes, the water was running in the sink.

Her heartbeat quickened. Something was definitely wrong.

She went in and saw no doctor, no patient. Someone had just left the faucet running. She quickly went over and shut it off, confused. Had Dr. Mauro just left here without turning off the faucet or light, or locking the door? Had he been in a rush?

"Dr. Mauro?" she called again, scanning the room.

Her breath caught when her eyes fell to the floor.

There was a man's scuffed dress shoe, there, behind the exam table. She craned her neck forward.

Not only a shoe, but a *leg*. A man.

"Dr. Mauro?" she tried again, recognizing the pants, the shirt as she moved forward, revealing more and more of him. Yes, it was the doctor. He was absolutely motionless, his eyes, open, nearly rolled back into his head. There was a little bit of froth at his mouth, and one hand still clutched at his collar, as if he'd been having trouble trying to breathe.

He was *definitely* having trouble now. He was dead.

Audrey leaned over and touched his skin of his hand. Cold and waxy. She put a hand over his eyes, but the lids stayed open. She staggered back against the wall and stifled a scream, then fumbled for her phone.

CHAPTER TWELVE

Audrey sat on the edge of a planter filled mostly with weeds at the front of the vet center, trying to keep her breathing normal. Nick sat at her ankles, providing quiet emotional support.

The same three police officers kept roaming in and out of the building, collecting evidence and speaking animatedly in Italian. Two, a man and a very pretty woman with long blonde hair in a ponytail, were young, almost as young as Vito, and the older one was old enough to be their mother. *She's probably my age,* Audrey thought sourly.

They were all dressed very neatly in blue, but something about them seemed much more like the Brady Bunch than CSI. As thorough as they were being, going in and out of the place, Audrey gathered they hadn't had to deal with much death during their time on the force.

As she waited patiently for them to ask questions, she yawned.

Forget about getting back to the hotel at a reasonable hour. Not that she would ever sleep now.

She shuddered as she thought of the body lying there on the linoleum. Poor man. He may have been an arrogant blowhard, but he didn't deserve to die. What had happened? Was it a heart attack? He was older, and obviously had a short temper, so that was probably it. Maybe he'd just been washing up when it happened.

An ambulance arrived, and two EMTs came out with a stretcher. She moved her legs to the side to let them pass in the narrow opening.

The older police officer approached her. Her bright red-dyed hair curled under her police officer's hat, and underneath the brim, her eyes were striking blue. Despite her angelic appearance, though, her voice was brusque, with only the hint of an accent. "Ms. Smart?"

"Doctor Smart. Yes?"

"I'm Officer Lorenzo. Uh. Hello."

"Hi."

"Bear with me, I'm—uh—this is obviously a new thing for us. You're the American who found the body?" she asked, paging through a notebook for a blank page. "Are you here on vacation?"

Audrey shook her head. "I'm here for work. I was called in by the town council to work on the stray problem. I'm a veterinarian. Same as Dr. Mauro."

The woman's eyes lit up. "Ah. That's not good, huh?"

Audrey shrugged. "It's not?"

The woman smiled. "Not today, I don't think. So you knew the deceased? You were friends? Coworkers?"

"No, we weren't friends. We weren't even coworkers. I only got to the island a day ago. I'd heard about him, of course. And I'd only met him once, earlier today."

"And why were you here at the vet center? After it was closed?"

Audrey yawned. "I just came by to . . ." Audrey stopped when she saw what the officer was holding, in a plastic evidence bag. "What is that?"

Officer Lorenzo held it up into the light of the streetlight. "Perhaps you can tell us. You didn't notice it near the body when you found it?"

She shook her head and looked closer. In addition to a syringe, there was also an empty bottle of pentobarbital.

It was a substance she knew very well, because it was used in the euthanasia of pets. She gulped.

The stone planter under her bottom suddenly felt uncomfortable. Audrey shifted.

"You do know what this is?" the officer prodded.

There was no use lying. Any veterinarian knew pentobarbital. "Of course. Are you saying that . . . he was injected with that?"

She nodded. "Appears so. What is it?"

"It's lethal, to animals, and to humans, in the right dose. It's used to put down animals. I don't understand. Was it a suicide?"

"Possibly. Or murder," she said, eyeing Audrey very closely. "We haven't ruled that out. We don't get murders at all in this town. Not at all. It's strange; you've only been here a few days and already you've found the first murder in Lipari in over fifty years."

"Or . . . suicide," she added. "Right?"

The officer ignored her. "No sign of struggle, so we think that it's someone who he knew."

"He knows himself," Audrey offered.

Ignoring her again, the officer said, "Not to mention that whoever murdered him clearly knew how to use pentobarbital, the correct dosage, where to administer it . . ."

"Well, I'm sure Dr. Mauro knows all that information fairly well . . ." she said weakly, knowing exactly what she was getting at. Again, she shifted, the familiar feelings settling over her as she avoided the officer's damning gaze.

Audrey was a suspect. Maybe their main suspect.

For a place that hadn't had a murder in fifty years, they were *awfully* quick to classify this as a homicide.

Officer Lorenzo went through her notes, looking a little confused. "Could you tell me . . . you said you met the doctor before?"

She nodded, wincing a little when she thought of what had happened between them. But there was no sense in trying to hide it. They'd had a full audience. It would come out eventually.

"Well, we'd had a bit of an altercation earlier in the day," she explained, only realizing when the words were out how bad it was. Maybe with her fighting words, she'd driven him to suicide? She didn't murder him, that much she knew. But he was an arrogant jerk. He probably had *tons* of enemies. "But I came here to offer an olive branch and see if there was some way we could clear the air."

"You did, hmm," the woman said, sitting down beside her, as if she was ready to pounce and pin her quarry. "What was your altercation about?"

Of course she'd narrow in on that. Like I'd be so upset at him calling me a "little girl" that I'd murder him. Ridiculous.

"It was all a misunderstanding, you see. I think he thought I was looking to cut in on his business, which wasn't the case," Audrey explained. "Like I said, the council hired me to work on the stray problem. I'm only here temporarily to get that under control. I was hoping to work with him, offer him recommendations, but he didn't want to hear them. I came back here, hoping to get him to listen to reason."

"And he wouldn't, and so you . . ."

"No!" she burst out. *Holy cow, are they ever going to stop?* "I never even talked to him! The last time I saw him alive was in that field across the street. When I found him in his office, he was already dead. It looked like he'd been dead a few hours."

"A few hours?" Now the officer tilted her head. "How did you know that?"

Audrey said, "Well, I am a doctor, Officer. And the mortises were already well on their way."

The officer hesitated. "The mortises?"

Audrey counted on her finger. "One, the body was cold. Yes, I touched it, to confirm he was dead. Two, rigor mortis had set in. I couldn't close his eyelids. I didn't look for livor mortis but those two facts alone signal he'd been dead more than two hours. You don't need a coroner for that."

The woman stared at her, dumbfounded. *Yes, these people have never worked a murder before.*

Finally, Officer Lorenzo said, "Nevertheless, the coroner is on his way."

"Of course. I wouldn't expect you to take my word for it," Audrey said, hugging herself. As the night wore on, it'd begun to get cold. "But I'll have you know that I spent the last three hours up at the animal shelter, and I have two witnesses who were with me the whole time, who can corroborate that fact."

Lorenzo wrote something down. "I'll need their information."

"Sure. It's Vito and Sabina. They're at the shelter at the top of the hill—I don't know what it's called, but it's the biggest one in the town."

"Hmm. And before then?"

"Before then? I was—" She stopped. She'd gone out after lunch to get some air, and ended up spending a few hours tracking down cats. "I was collecting strays, out near the beach."

"Can anyone confirm that?"

"No . . ." she said, a familiar feeling gripping her throat. She hadn't seen a soul. She looked down at her scratched hands and added weakly, "But I got these scratches from one of them. I caught four of them. I can show you?"

The officer held up a hand. "And you're staying where?"

"At the Hotel Lipari."

"You'll have to stay here, Miss Smart, in case we need you for anything else. You understand, right?"

She didn't feel like correcting her to *Doctor* again, so she nodded.

Officer Lorenzo gave her a business card. "If you think of anything, please give me a call. All right?"

"Sure." She'd been through this drill before. Four victims. This was the fourth dead body she'd found in Italy, in as many months. Had to be some kind of record. Or the result of really bad luck. "Of course. If there is anything you need, I am happy to help."

The officer nodded and headed back inside. Audrey forgot to ask if she was dismissed. And she so desperately wanted to go back to her

63

hotel, take a bath, and rest. The two other officers were excitedly nudging one another and giggling. Audrey couldn't shake the feeling that they were watching this more like it was an episode of *CSI* than an actual murder investigation.

She shivered as the EMTs came out with the stretcher, the body covered in a white sheet. Even that sight didn't strike the officers with the appropriate amount of somberness. They watched the body as it was loaded into the back of the ambulance, then one whispered something to the other, and they both burst out laughing.

Wait . . . were they flirting? A man had just been murdered, and they were falling in love?

Great. Inexperienced officers who weren't totally focused on the case. How many ways could they screw this investigation up?

She didn't want to find out. She stood up. "Excuse me, Officer. Am I excused to leave?"

He looked at her as if he'd never seen her before. Even though he was the first one on the scene. Even though she'd been the one to show him the body. He wrinkled his nose and said, *"Chi sei?"* Who are you?

Audrey rolled her eyes. This was going to be bad. If she had to wait for them to solve this, she might never get back to her clinic in Mussomeli.

She'd have to start looking for answers herself.

CHAPTER THIRTEEN

Audrey was absolutely numb by the time she got back to the Hotel Lipari at nearly eleven in the evening. It was utterly dark on the street, but the red and blue lights from the police cars seemed to reflect off every surface in the neighborhood, and several people were standing outside their homes, trying to see what had happened.

She trudged through the door and climbed the stairs, trying to avoid anyone who might have seen her at the scene and would ask her what had happened. Right then, she didn't even want a bath. She was too tired to think of anything but bed.

When she opened the door, her phone buzzed with a message. It was from Brina, asking how her trip was going and showing her a picture of a new dish she'd made for dinner. Audrey hadn't eaten much all day, but right then, she didn't think she had the energy to get her mouth to chew.

She climbed into bed, still wearing that day's clothes, and pulled the covers up to her chin, expecting that sleep would grab her the second her head hit the pillow.

The air conditioning thrummed, filling the room with cool, pleasant air. Outside, the distant horns of ships in the harbor sounded. After about ten minutes of lying there, she opened her eyes and stared up at the ceiling.

She was wide awake.

Of course.

Dr. Mauro was dead. And once again, she'd found the body. Once again, she was a suspect. How did she always get herself into these things?

But now, things were different. Now, she felt like she had more experience than the officers in charge of handling the case. Officer Lorenzo seemed nice enough, but she didn't have the know-how. And those two lovebirds weren't going to be any help.

They should check with his past clients. He has a lot of misdiagnoses, she thought. *Probably a lot of unhappy customers.*

They should. But *would* they?

That was the question. They'd think of that, right? Maybe. Hopefully, they would, instead of focusing all their efforts on Audrey.

She sat up in bed and turned on the light. She grabbed her purse from the night table and found the business card. She dialed the number, waiting for an answer. A sleepy voice suddenly answered. "Lorenzo."

"Hi. This is Audrey Smart, the doctor who found Dr. Mauro's body. I'm sorry to bother you so late but I had an idea I wanted to run past you."

"Miss Smart, go on."

"Well, a couple of animals I saw had recently been seen by Dr. Mauro. And there is talk that he may have accidentally misdiagnosed some of them. So I was thinking—"

"Yes, yes. We're already doing that."

Audrey paused. "Are you? Because—"

"We appreciate your help, but please let us do the investigating. The last thing we need is a suspect muddling up the investigation, and—"

"But I'm trying to tell you that—"

"I know very well what you're up to. You're trying to clear your name."

"No. I—"

"Why can't you sleep? Do you have a guilty conscience?"

Audrey's jaw dropped. The nerve of this lady. "No! Of course no. I'm just trying to—"

"Miss Smart. Do you have any additional evidence or something else you remembered from the scene?"

"No, I was just—"

"Then I thank you for your time. But we'll be in touch if we need you."

Click.

Okay, that was rather rude. Audrey sat up in bed, listening to the dead air. Did they really have it under control? Audrey didn't want to doubt. Dr. Mauro had doubted her abilities, based solely on her appearance. She didn't want to cast the same doubt on this police force for theirs.

But she couldn't help it. Especially knowing that the longer they took, the longer she'd be stuck on the island. If she couldn't get back, would she lose her clinic?

The bottom line was, she didn't trust the police force to pull out all the stops to find the killer as quickly as possible. Only Audrey would be able to do that.

*

That morning, Audrey felt like the dead.

If only she'd slept like it.

Instead, as exhausted as she'd been, she hadn't slept at all. Now she was going on two nights with barely any sleep.

She crawled out of bed and took a shower, hoping it would help revive her. Then she ran the coffee maker and got dressed, hoping coffee would do the trick. But by the time she was ready to set out, she was still so tired, she could barely see.

She'd promised Vito and Sabina she'd be at the shelter early that morning, but the murder hung too heavily on her mind. She knew she'd never be able to get the day's work done with the strays unless she did a little bit of digging into Dr. Mauro's murder first.

And that meant checking in with some of Dr. Mauro's past patients.

Short of breaking into his center, which she really didn't want to do, she decided her best bet was to talk to Fabio the Mastiff's owner, Marco. He'd mentioned something about Dr. Mauro not being the greatest of vets. Maybe he had some ideas.

She met Nick outside, where he'd likely been curled up in an alley somewhere. He looked well-rested, bright-eyed and bushy-tailed. If only she could say the same for herself. "Hi, bub." She yawned again.

He tilted his head as if to say, *And now what is wrong with you?*

"So much," she muttered, shivering as the early morning cool breeze off the sea hit her arms. "Why is it that you don't ever stop me from putting my foot in it, huh, Nick?"

He simply scampered ahead of her.

It was a good thing that Marco's house was right down the street, because Audrey was so tired, her feet felt like cinderblocks as she lifted them, plodding along toward his place. When she got to the front stoop, she leaned against the side of the building and knocked lethargically.

No answer.

Audrey's shoulders slumped. She looked back at the hotel, which seemed to be a million miles away, even though it was right on the corner. Everything around her looked like a suitable bed. Funny how when she'd had the opportunity to, she hadn't been able to sleep a wink. Now, her eyelids sagged. She just wanted to lie down and take a little nap . . .

HONK!

She was startled upright by the sound of Vito's car, pulling up to the curb beside her. He rolled down the window and grinned at her. "Doing a follow-up?"

"No, I uh—"

"I've got news for you," he said, smiling smugly. "You will not believe it."

She only hesitated a second. It wasn't a bed, but it was close enough, and a better option than collapsing on the sidewalk, which was very possible, with the way she was feeling. *I've got news, too,* she thought as she sunk into the seat. Even though the vinyl was warm and sticky, it felt good. She yawned and closed her eyes, and sleep nearly took her right then.

Vito took off, nearly giving her whiplash. "So, how was your night? You didn't sleep good?"

She yawned again. It was like every time she opened her mouth, a yawn came out. She couldn't control it. "I have had better nights. You said you had news."

"Yeah, I do. Get this. You know Dr. Mauro?"

She turned to look at him, now more alert. News certainly traveled fast in small towns. Did everyone know? "Let me guess. He's dead."

Vito's mouth hung open. "So you heard?"

"I was there."

"What? Are you kidding me?" He wiped his hair from his eyes and looked at her. His expression was more like awe than fear. "You're like a witness? How'd that happen?"

"I'm not a witness. I just found the body."

"Seriously?"

"Yes. Remember that altercation I had with him? Well, after you dropped me off at the hotel, I decided to go to his office and clear the air with him. And I found him in the exam room. Dead."

Now Vito looked like he'd won the lottery. "No kidding. Holy cow. What happened? Was there a lot of blood? I heard they think there was foul play involved."

"The police do, yes. And maybe there is. I suggested suicide, because no, there wasn't a lot of blood. He was injected with pentobarbital."

"You mean the euthanasia medication?"

68

She nodded. "Which he obviously had on hand. But for some reason, the police don't believe that. Even though they told me there's never been another murder here in fifty years, they seem to think it's a murder."

"Holy freaking cow," he said again. "No wonder you didn't sleep."

"Right. So I'm sorry if I'm not thinking too much about the clinic right now," she said. "The police seem a little uneducated about these things, and they're actually thinking I might have committed the murder."

"You? No way! Besides, you were with me yesterday."

Audrey appreciated the vote of confidence, but she didn't think his opinion would carry weight with the police. She said, "They seem to think I could've done it while I was off collecting strays after lunch. Remember? I was alone."

"Still. You? How could they think that?"

"And I have a little experience in amateur sleuthing, so—"

"You do?" He gave her a doubtful look.

"Yeah, I actually . . . solved a couple of murders in Mussomeli." When he started to look impressed, she added, "It was really no big deal."

"On top of saving strays, one animal at a time? What other superpowers do you have?"

Audrey shook her head. "Like I said. It was not a big deal. But I'm afraid the police aren't listening to me. I tried to tell them that for possible suspects, they should be looking into the misdiagnoses that I'd heard about, but they pretty much stonewalled me and told me they didn't want my help. Guess it makes sense that they wouldn't want my help, since they think I'm some *dastardly murderer.*" She ended the sentence with a foreboding voice and wiggled her fingers together like an evil genius.

"Oh, so that's why you were at Marco's place, huh? You thought he might have some idea as to who did this?"

"Yeah. It was a start." She shrugged. "But you said a lot of people were unhappy with him?"

He nodded.

"So short of going through his files, that was the best I could do."

She yawned again. Her eyes felt heavier than ever, until suddenly, with no warning whatsoever, Vito slammed on the brakes.

Her eyes bulged. Her neck ached from the whiplash. Massaging it, she looked over at him, her voice raised in alarm. "What. The. H—"

"I have an idea."

"I have one, too, Vito. How about 'not get into an accident'?"

"No. We should go over to his place. Check around. I bet we can get in."

"*We?*" She shook her head. "No way. I'm not dragging you into this."

"You're not dragging me into anything," he said, doing a U-turn in the middle of the road. "I'm doing it of my own free will."

"Wait. Where are you going?" she asked, stiffening as he hung a right and a sinking suspicion settled over her. *He's going to the vet clinic. He's going to break us in and get us both arrested.*

"Relax. We're just going to check it out and see what's going on there."

She gave him a doubtful look. "You're not going to try to break in?"

He shrugged. "Not yet. Let's just see what we're dealing with."

"Vito? Not *yet*. Never. Promise me. You could get in so much trouble."

He didn't promise. He simply waggled his eyebrows and grinned mischievously.

Audrey wrapped her hand even tighter around the handle on the door. *This is not a good idea.*

They pulled up the street and he settled into a crawl as they came to the clinic. She felt like a criminal, casing the joint. Remarkably, there was no police tape there, no police presence at all, nothing to alert anyone to the fact that a murder had taken place there.

"Look at that. I could just mosey on in there with a sick . . ." He looked over his shoulder at Nick. ". . . fox, and pretend I didn't know anything about the murder."

He grinned.

Audrey shook her head. "This has 'bad idea' written all over it." She looked back at the building on the corner. It was strange to see it so deserted, considering how busy it had been last night. "What if we go there and touch something and they look for fingerprints? Then I'll really get tied to the murder. And so will you."

He pulled to the curb. "No, we won't. First, you were already in there, right? You found the body, so your fingerprints are already everywhere. And secondly . . ." He reached into the seat behind her and pulled out the box of latex gloves. "Good thing we came prepared."

"Vito. No. Absolutely not." She shook her head vigorously.

"You're right. The police are bumbling idiots. You're going to leave the investigation in their hands?"

"I don't know . . ." she hedged, but even then, she knew he was right. What was most important now was finding the killer. *She* had more experience than the police force on the island. And if they were going to continue to stonewall her and not accept her suggestions, what else could she do?

He handed her the gloves and slipped his own on. "Come on. You might be an expert in animals, but this is where I'm the pro. Trust me."

He stepped out of the car and jogged across the street. She gathered Nick into her arms and hurried after him. When she got there, he tried the front door. It opened, but the one in the vestibule was locked. A quick glance through the glass door confirmed the place was empty.

Audrey sighed in relief. "Oh well, too bad. Can we go now?"

"One second."

They went back outside. Nick wriggled from her grip and disappeared behind some bushes. Audrey made a beeline for the street where the car was parked. "Time to go," she sang under her breath.

Vito hesitated, scanning the area around the building. "I have a better idea."

She shook her head. "Oh no. Please. No."

He pushed his hair off his face and winked at her. "Follow me."

Before she could protest any more, he stuck his hands in his pockets and looked both ways as he nonchalantly backed toward the alley behind the building. In a blink, he slipped inside.

She hesitated. *The most important thing now is finding the killer,* she reminded herself.

Slightly less gracefully, with a lot less composure, Audrey followed suit.

She found herself in an alley so small, she practically grazed both walls with her shoulders. They were covered with a thick mass of ivy. The floor was brick, with a narrow gulley of murky water flowing out of it toward the street. Though it was a bright, sunny morning, the walls and vegetation blocked out a good deal of sun. She had to squint to see Vito standing in front of her.

He was smirking as he motioned with his chin. "Here we are."

She looked up to see a window. It was covered in a dirty screen and rather high up on the wall. From what she could tell, it was the window that she'd seen in the waiting room. "Don't tell me—"

"Why not? I've broken into a lot more secure places than this."

71

"Fantastic. But I thought you turned over a new leaf?"

"I did. I'm helping the good guys now." He reached up to fiddle with the lock, then looked at her. "You have a . . . that. Can I borrow that?"

He pointed to the hair clip holding the stray short hairs off her forehead. She unclipped it and handed it to him.

"Awesome." He took it, bent it in a certain way, and fiddled with the latch again. As nervous as she was, she was also a little impressed. Because whatever he was doing, he was doing it in darkness, under stress. She kept glancing toward the street, thinking she might pass out. "And *voila*."

The hinges creaked as he tilted the screen up, then gave the window a few shoves. It budged a little each time. Before long, there was a narrow opening.

"Now what?" she asked, not liking where this was heading.

"I'll give you a boost. You go in."

"What? No! You're not coming with me?"

He started counting off on his fingers. "One, if I give you a boost, who gives me a boost? Two, you need someone to keep watch. Three, there's no way I'm fitting through that window."

She glanced up at it, worry creasing her forehead. Taking a deep breath, she let it out slowly, psyching herself up for it.

"Okay, okay. Fine. Give me a boost before I lose my courage."

CHAPTER FOURTEEN

I can't believe I'm doing this, Audrey thought as she stepped onto Vito's laced fingers and he boosted her up to the window. As he lifted her, she grabbed a hold of the window ledge and slid in the narrow opening.

Unfortunately, sliding in headfirst meant that her head would be the first thing to hit the ground on the other side. And Vito was being a lot quicker about shoving her over than she would've liked.

"Hold on!" she cried over her shoulder as he pushed her through. Yes, it was the waiting room, as she'd expected, but she had other things on her mind at the moment. In particular, how she was going to wriggle herself down from the ledge without doing a faceplant.

She nearly lost her balance, but then grabbed ahold of the wall to steady herself. Sliding her hands down it, she fisted a chair's armrests in both hands and slowly wormed her way onto it. When her feet were the last thing clinging to the window ledge, she tried to bring them down, one at a time, to cushion the fall, but the chair slipped out from under her and she went sliding, landing on the floor with a bang. Her elbows took the brunt of the fall.

"Ouch."

"You okay?"

The threadbare carpet her chin was resting on was so covered in dust bunnies, it was amazing the floor was as hard as it felt. She stifled a sneeze. As she rolled to the side, everything hurt. She faced the aquarium, where two goldfish swam, unconcerned with her predicament. Then she looked around the rest of the dim, cramped waiting area.

Nobody was there. That was good, at least.

"No," she called back, massaging a sore hip as she rolled all the way over and climbed to her feet.

"Really?" He sounded worried.

"I'm fine," she muttered, as suddenly, something appeared in the window. She sucked in a breath, sure it was someone coming to arrest her. But it was just Nick, who stood there for a moment, gauging his next steps, before gracefully scurrying across the window ledge, hopping to a book shelf, then to a chair back, then finally to the ground. Audrey shook her head. "I wish you could read, Nick. Then *you* could've done this for us. Come on."

"If you hear me whistle," Vito called, "that means someone's coming, and to get out. Okay?"

A shiver went down her back. She really didn't want to think about that. "Whistle? Like how?"

He whistled, like he was catcalling a pretty girl on the sidewalk. *Whoo-whooooo.*

"Oh. Okay." She wiped her sweaty palms on her khaki shorts. "How do I get out?"

"Just the same way you got in."

Oh, god, no, she thought with dread. But it would be easier. She could just climb on the chair back, and hopefully, Vito would be there to catch her. *Think about that when you're done. Right now, you have work to do.*

"Got it."

The door to the rooms in the back of the building was open. She quickly passed through, stopping every time she heard a noise, sure she was hearing a whistle. But when she paused, she realized it was only her imagination. *Get a hold of yourself, Audrey.*

She purposely avoided the examination room where she'd found Dr. Mauro's body and crept to the second door. Pushing it open, she found an office, with a desk and a chair, and a pile of papers and folders that seemed to be in no order whatsoever. No filing cabinet.

Turning around, she saw the receptionist's area. The entire back of that room was made up of several giant wall-sized, walnut filing cabinets.

Jackpot.

She rushed over to it and opened the closest drawer. It didn't glide open easily; it rumbled on a squeaky track, since the cabinet looked like something from the nineteenth century. When she peered in, hundreds and hundreds of manila folders with colored tabs stared back at her.

Where to begin?

She pulled one out from the center of the cabinet, for someone named Avila. A cat with conjunctivitis. No problems there. Then a dog with allergies. She pulled out a few more, going through each, trying to find some red flags. But despite his messy, smeared handwriting (perhaps he was left-handed) and penchant for dripping some kind of food or drink on the files, since there were many sticky droplets on them, there was nothing to write home about.

She noticed, as she went, that the files were not sorted by year, but alphabetically. Newer files were mixed in with older ones, and it was easy to tell which was which, because the older files contained faded, yellowing paper. Some of them dated back to the early eighties. They were the more thorough, neater ones, Audrey noticed. But though the newer of his reports were very terse, his handwriting a little shakier, everything seemed to be in order.

She looked around. No computers. There was, in fact, a vinyl-covered typewriter, sitting in the corner. *He doesn't keep any of his files online. They're all in here. No wonder it's such a mess. Dr. Mauro is old-school.*

She went back to the file and pulled out a thicker one, for the Bustantes. They had a pet golden retriever, and had been in to see the doctor only last year. It was mostly in Italian, so she did her best to translate, but from what she could tell, the poor pup had only lived a few years. Cancer, it said, which was not unusual, since golden retrievers were prone to the disease. What was unusual was the dog's age. Only four? The disease continued to spread, though, so Dr. Mauro eventually had to put the dog down.

Audrey lifted out the X-ray film that was included in the folder and held the images up to the minimal light from the window, looking for the telltale signs of tumors.

But she could see none.

In fact, the animal's body was completely clear and healthy. He had possibly a bit of a bone density problem which might have contributed to his ill health, but like Marco's Mastiff, that could've been rectified with a better diet.

Audrey cringed. Had Dr. Mauro seriously misdiagnosed a healthy animal and sent him to his death?

She pushed such horrible thoughts away. Veterinarians were human, after all. Science was imperfect. Doctors could make mistakes. Or maybe there was something in the X-rays that she didn't see.

"Poor pup," she whispered, going to the next folder.

This one was a dog with hip dysplasia. From the X-rays, yes, the beginning signs were there, but according to the file, he'd performed euthanasia on the dog only a month after diagnosis. Another one, with kidney disease, that he'd dismissed as lethargy until the animal had passed on.

A sickness swelled in Audrey's gut. Unless she was missing something in the translation, Dr. Mauro was clearly euthanasia-happy and too quick to diagnosis without the proper tests.

She pulled out a few more recent folders, noticing the same thing, and piled them together. There was a photocopier in the corner of the office that she could use. But the file folders were something like a rabbit hole, and one of Audrey's favorite parts of the job was diagnosing patients, so she found herself getting a little lost in them and forgetting where she was.

It all came flooding back, though, when she heard a strange whistle. *What kind of crazy bird is that?* she wondered for a split second, before she remembered.

That was Vito's signal.

It meant someone was coming.

CHAPTER FIFTEEN

With no time to lose, Audrey grabbed the pile of folders and raced to the reception area. As she did, she saw shadows behind the glass in the front vestibule. Someone was standing there, going through keys, trying to find the right one to open the door.

Meanwhile, just outside, Vito whistled, again and again, like a bird caught in a hurricane. Audrey eyed the window, her escape. She didn't have the time. Even if she jumped up and dove through the window with all the grace of an acrobat, the person at the door would be inside in seconds.

Looking around for an alternative plan, she quickly spotted it.

There was a hat rack near the door, covered with a number of jackets and hats. It didn't quite occur to her why there were so many jackets on the rack, since it was still very warm in late September, and obviously there were no patients to be seen. But it was full of them, which was the one break Audrey got. Holding the folders to her chest, she edged toward it and slid in the small space between the hat rack and the wall.

She closed her eyes and said a little prayer as a second later, there was the sound of the key turning in the lock, and the door opening.

The coats had clearly been there a while, because they smelled like dust and mothballs. Audrey stifled a sneeze as she peered between them, at the male police officer who'd been there last night. He walked in, gnawing loudly on something, an apple, maybe, and strolled past her, not even looking her way. He went through the doors to the back room, completely oblivious to her presence.

Without wasting a beat, Audrey slipped out the other side of the coat rack, nearest the door, pushed it open, and escaped into the warm morning. When she got there, she looked around, sure one of the other officers would be waiting there, to snap some handcuffs on her. But the street was empty.

She went around to the alley and casually peered down it. Vito was still there, still whistling. She snapped her fingers. He caught sight of her and followed her down the street.

When they were far enough away, he caught up with her. "What did you get? You find anything?"

"I found a *load* of stuff," she said, holding up the files. "Including a man named Davide Bustante, whose pet golden retriever was euthanized by Dr. Mauro a month ago because he was suffering from cancer. But guess what? He didn't have cancer."

"Yeah?" He looked at the folders in her hands. "Are all of those . . ."

She nodded. "All of them are misdiagnoses, and fairly new cases that resulted in the animal's death. There's a lot more where this came from, but it's a start."

Vito stopped walking suddenly. Audrey turned back to look at him. "Bustante. I know that guy. He works at the gym down by the harbor. He's . . . interesting."

"Interesting good or interesting bad?" Audrey asked, but she could already see the answer by the constipated look on his face. "What's wrong with him?"

"Let's just say I wouldn't put it past him to murder someone who killed his best friend," Vito said, raking his hands through his hair. "But let's go."

"Hold on," Audrey said. "Gallo hired me to help with the stray problem. I haven't done anything to help today. Maybe you should go back to the clinic and help your Nonna. I'm sure she has a lot to do. Tell her I'll be there as soon as I talk to this man."

He grinned. "Bustante doesn't speak English, so you need me," he announced.

"All right," she said with a shrug. "Lead the way."

*

Audrey had passed *Palestra Bustante,* right at the harbor front, when she first arrived on the ferry, but she hadn't known what it was until now. She peered inside the small storefront and saw the gym mats, mirrored walls, weight benches, and large racks full of huge dumbbells and weights. A few very large, muscular men were standing in the front window, lifting what looked like cartoonishly large bar bells and grunting as sweat poured down their brows.

When Audrey walked in, her nostrils flared, accosted with the saline scent of fresh sweat. The few men there scoured her with their eyes like she was a piece of meat. The air seemed charged with steroids

78

and testosterone. This wasn't the juice-bar-and-elliptical-machine type of gym she knew of from Boston. This was for some seriously *scary*-looking dudes.

No wonder Vito had warned her. Some of these guys had thighs the circumference of Vito's entire torso.

"Lovely," she whispered to him, just as a tiny puppy barked, announcing their arrival.

The second it bounded up to her, Audrey felt a thousand times more at ease. That was the usual effect animals had on her. As she leaned down to pet it, she realized it was a tiny version of the golden retriever she'd seen in Bustante's files. "Hi there, baby. Who are you?"

A loud voice boomed from the back of the room, behind the various weightlifting equipment. She grasped a few words from the rapid-fire Italian—the puppy's name was Picco, the gym was running a special, and would Vito like a membership application? His tone wasn't solicitous, like he wanted them to join . . . he sounded more doubtful as if he already knew they'd have their work cut out for them.

When he appeared, Audrey understood why. He looked like Mr. Clean, right down to the gold earring. He was bald, wearing a tank top that showed off his massive muscles and trim waist. The only thing was, he wasn't smiling.

Audrey said, "No, we don't want an app—"

Vito began to speak over her, translating her thoughts into Italian. *No, we wanted to ask you a few questions about your visit to Dr. Mauro.*

Bustante's eyes narrowed, shifted between the two of them. "Mauro? *Che vuoi?*" What do you want?

Audrey said, "Did he meet with Dr. Mauro? Did Dr. Mauro tell him that his dog was sick? Did he—"

Vito held out a hand and spoke to him. Bustante nodded and spoke some more, gesticulating wildly. "What is he saying?"

Vito said, "He's saying that yes, this dog, Picco, is Picco junior, Picco senior died a month ago. He had cancer and was very ill, according to Mauro. One day he was fine, the next day, the doctor said he was too far gone and needed to be put down."

Audrey frowned. Euthanasia was something she didn't take lightly. She always tried to find an alternative method. It was a last resort. And unless the animal was in substantial pain, it was never something that she rushed into. The pet owners were always prepared for it, because it

79

was an important part of the process. "And Picco senior was only four years old. So he didn't seem sick at all?"

Vito translated, and Bustante shook his head. Then his eyes narrowed. "*Che? Chi sei?*" Who are you?

Audrey completely understood what Vito meant: This man looked like *Heads are gonna roll* was the motto he lived his life by. A vein bulged on the side of his neck, angry and on the verge of bursting. That couldn't have be good. If she were looking for guilty parties based on temperament alone, Davide Bustante would be at the top of the list.

Time to defuse the situation.

"*Signore Bustante*," she said, as sweetly as she could. "*Scusi*. We didn't mean to disturb you. I'm a veterinarian. I was just conducting a survey and wanted to see if you were happy with your level of care?"

Vito translated. The man's featured softened, but he shook his head. "Dr. Mauro. . . *bastardo. Sono felice che sia morto.*"

Audrey's eyes widened. Vito went to translate, but she held up a hand. She knew what that meant. *I'm glad he's dead.* "So he knows?"

Vito nodded. "Apparently." Then he asked, in Italian, *How did you find out?*

The man snorted and replied something about how there are no secrets in a town this small. All of Lipari knows. Then he narrowed his eyes again and said something that Audrey didn't understand. She looked at Vito.

Vito backed away and muttered, "He says if we don't get out of here and stop snooping, he's going to call the police." Then Vito seemed to have second thoughts. He said something about Picco to Davide.

Davide nodded and his face fell. For a moment, he looked like he might cry. Then he leaned down and picked up his puppy and said something, again, that Audrey could barely make out.

Vito nodded solemnly. Then he said to Audrey. "I think we should go."

"But . . .What did he say?" Audrey whispered.

"I'll tell you when we're outside," he said, still eyeing him and trying to nudge her toward the door.

Eventually, she gave in and followed him out into the bright sun. "Well?"

"He said that he tried to sue Mauro, but the local judge is a friend of Mauro's and the case was dismissed. So there's no love lost there."

"Aha!" Audrey said, eyeing him through the storefront. He was eyeing her right back, looking absolutely guilty as sin. "Why did you make me leave? I could've asked him more—"

"Because he said he was in Messina yesterday for the whole day. He only got back last night."

"He did?" Her spirits plummeted. "He could be lying."

Vito shook his head. "I don't think so. He said he was at a wedding and that there are a hundred people who could vouch for his whereabouts and that he didn't get home until midnight."

She sighed. "Oh."

That meant that, for all their crazy, dangerous escapades today, they were at a dead end.

She walked toward his car, her stomach swirling with a combination of relief and dread. "Come on. Let's go, Vito. We have some animals to take care of."

CHAPTER SIXTEEN

Audrey was lying on the beach, wriggling her toes in the warm water, the sun hot on her face. She had a tropical drink in her hand, a buff waiter at her beck and call, and no cares in the world. In the distance, seagulls squawked, and every so often, a cool breeze caressed her face. It was heaven, until . . .

"Wake up."

She squeezed her eyes tighter, trying to ignore the command.

"Audrey. Wake up." The voice was more insistent this time.

She blinked and found herself in Vito's car, with Nick and Vito both staring at her. Her cheek was pressed against her shoulder at an unnatural angle, and a line of drool dripped from her chin. She swiped at it and looked around. "What—where are we?"

"The shelter. It's after one. We have to finish the check-ups on the new cats we brought in yesterday."

"Oh, right." The fantasy popped in her head. As much as she loved the job of caring for animals, she had to admit, she liked that dream a lot better. To be sitting there, with no pressing engagements, no murder investigation going on . . .

The murder investigation.

"Ugh." She rubbed her sore neck, thinking of everything they'd done that day. From breaking and entering, to interviewing Davide Bustante and a number of the other names from the files she'd collected, they'd been all over the island. And they had absolutely nothing to show for it. Her stomach swam with the realization. "That was a waste of time, wasn't it?"

Vito shrugged. "It depends on how you look at it. It's like Edison, finding two thousand ways how not to make a light bulb. We just found four people who couldn't have killed Dr. Mauro."

She laughed bitterly. "I hope we don't have to do that two thousand times. I can't take it," she said, yawning and sitting up in the front passenger's seat. Sure enough, the shelter stood in front of them. She must've fallen asleep after their last visit to the old lady with the dog with kidney disease, because it all felt like a faraway dream. It was amazing that Vito's crazy driving hadn't woken her up once.

She pulled on the door handle and got out, still rubbing her sore neck. That catnap had only served to make her feel more exhausted. As they went around to the front of the building, she noticed Councilman Gallo's car parked out front.

Great. Just what I need right now. An interview with the boss. I wonder if he's going to think I murdered Mauro, too, she thought, smoothing her hair back into a ponytail and letting it fall neatly behind her back. She paused in front of the window and inspected her reflection. She had enough bags under her eyes for a trip to Japan. *Let's get this over with.*

She went inside just as Gallo was unleashing a series of robust sneezes. She found him rushing out of the kennel room, eyes watering. "Oh, Dottore Smart!" he said, relieved. "Thank goodness. I need to talk to you."

"Would you like to go outside?" she said.

He sneezed. "Yes. *Grazie.* That would be best."

She told Vito to get started tending to the animals and headed outside with the ailing councilman. When she got there, before he could turn around, she said, "I know why you're here."

He turned, a confused expression on his face. "And why is that?"

"Dr. Mauro. I'm sure you've heard."

He nodded, his face full of regret. "Indeed. It's a shame, what happened to him. Lipari is quiet place. I can't believe it happened."

She swallowed. "That's why I wanted to let you know. I understand the reservations you must have about working with me and trusting me to care for these animals. But I wanted to reassure you that as long as I can, my focus has been and will always be on the animals first."

Confusion darkened his expression. "Reservations?" He started to laugh. "Oh, no, Dottore Smart. Of course, it was a shock, but I have no reservations where you are concerned. None at all."

She rocked from her heels to her toes. "You mean, you don't think that I killed him?"

He laughed even harder. "Now why would I think such a thing?"

"Well, first, because the *police* seem to think it was me. I suppose they think I was jealous and wanted to take his position from him. And since I found the body, I know how to administer the pentobarbital, and they don't have any other suspects . . ."

"Ah. Well—" He paused. "*You* found the body? Why on earth were you—"

83

"I had had a bit of a fight with him a few hours before, and I stopped by his clinic to clear the air with him. Not to kill him."

He stared at her, a peculiar expression on his face, almost as if he was suddenly deciding the police were right. Maybe she'd said too much. It was better when he thought she could do no wrong. "That's . . . astonishing."

"Yes. But the fact remains . . . I didn't kill him."

"Oh, I know that, dear," he said, waving it off. "I've seen enough mysteries to know that the person who finds the body and calls it in is very rarely the killer. Why stick around and wait to be caught? Right?"

"Oh." That made sense. "Yes, I guess you're right. I never thought about that."

"And so you wanted to clear the air with him? You know what a stubborn fool he can be?"

She nodded. "I realized that if the animal control problem in Lipari was ever going to get better, I needed to reason with him, since he's all this town has, once I leave."

Gallo held up a finger. "Which brings me to my visit to you. The reason I was here, my dear, was because I was hoping that you might consider relocating your clinic to Lipari. Considering we're now in dire need of a veterinarian."

She blinked. She hadn't been expecting that one. "What?"

"I know, I know. But we're up against a wall here. You understand. And we need the help."

She understood that, but it still sounded rather crass. Dr. Mauro had been dead less than twenty-four hours, and here they were, already trying to get a replacement? "Oh, yes, but—"

"You'll think about it?"

It would be easy enough to give it all up for the greener grass on the other side. But then she thought of the friends she'd made in Mussomeli. The many pets she'd grown to love over the past few months. Not to mention Concetta, G, the café owner who was so sweet to her, and of course, Mason. She'd left too many things unresolved. Though the speed bumps along the line were many, her work there was far from done. She shook her head. "I would, but I don't see how I possibly can. Back in Mussomeli—"

"We received a generous grant to support the animal control effort. That's where your pay came from. But there's much more planned. We could arrange a new clinic, state-of-the-art equipment, whatever you need. How about it?"

"It sounds really amazing, but—" She paused. A lot of her troubles in Mussomeli revolved around never having enough money. Her home was still a mess, the clinic was a work in progress, and she was constantly watching her bank account. Besides, it wasn't like there was anyone in Mussomeli missing her so badly.

She cringed as she thought of Mason, prancing off with that gorgeous girl of his. He'd toyed with her for months, making her think he was interested, only to play her for a fool, the jerk. Lipari could be a fresh start. A new beginning . . .

He cleared his throat, startling her out of her thoughts. "Well, if you can think of another one of your colleagues, please let me know," he said, shaking his head. "Or maybe you change your mind? Think on it and see."

She smiled. "Okay. Maybe."

"Maybe is good!" he said.

I doubt it, she thought. *I've been here less than a day and already I'm a murder suspect. At least in Mussomeli, I went several days before that happened.*

She almost laughed at her bad luck. Not to mention, it wouldn't be all roses and sunshine, here either. For one thing, she'd have to deal with an island of people who might not trust her, simply because of the bad reputation of her predecessor. That would be a hard thing to shake, being under the thumb of a euthanasia-happy man. There were probably plenty of residents who refused to see the vet when their pet really needed it, simply because—

Suddenly, something struck her. "Councilman Gallo, I have a question for you," she said, plowing forward without waiting for him to respond. "You mentioned that there were other solutions to the stray problem presented to the council, right?"

"That's correct."

"Who else provided those solutions? Did Dr. Mauro have any ideas?"

He nodded slowly. "He did indeed. None that any of us were very keen on. That was why we decided to look for outside help. We never took his plan very seriously, and, well . . . it angered many of the locals who deemed it inhumane."

"What was it?" she asked, though she had a pretty good idea already.

"Well, he wanted to perform mass euthanasia on the cats. Kill almost all of the ones in the shelters, and poison the ones that were running free."

Audrey's blood ran cold. Even though Gallo said it with a great deal of regret in his voice, she could hardly imagine, as a veterinarian, advocating for anything so cruel. She shuddered. "That's awful. I'm glad you looked into other avenues."

He smiled. "I'm glad, too."

But the fact remained that Dr. Mauro had been murdered by the same euthanasia drug that he was planning to use on the stray pet population. He had a number of enemies who saw him as inhumane. Maybe someone out there, some crazed pet lover or a person who really wanted to save all the animals, had decided he deserved a dose of his own medicine?

If that was the case, only one question remained: Did she know anyone who fit that description?

As she turned back to the shelter, the answer hit her straight between the eyes.

CHAPTER SEVENTEEN

Audrey's knees wobbled as she went inside to the kennels.

As she walked inside, deep in thought, she couldn't shake the strange feeling that overtook her. Sabina had mentioned something about a cat she had owned that Dr. Mauro had supposedly killed, years ago. Sabina loved animals like her own babies. Sabina had transformed her home into a refuge for stray cats. If anyone on the island of Lipari could be called a stray pet lover, it was Sabina.

And there was a very good chance that a pet lover had killed Dr. Mauro over his unorthodox animal control tactics.

That meant that, as much as she didn't want to believe it . . .

Sabina had motive.

Sabina wasn't in the kennel area when she arrived. She hesitated in the doorway, watching Vito pour food into bowls for the cats. He was a good kid. Sabina may have been a little crazy, but she was all he had.

The thought of her being locked away in prison for murder tore at Audrey's heart. She felt so sick over it that she didn't notice Vito staring at her curiously. "Everything okay, Audrey?"

She nodded and swallowed. "Yep. Fine."

"'Cause pardon my saying so, but you look like you're gonna hurl." He smirked.

Truthfully, she did feel like she was going to be sick. She swallowed the bile in her throat and shook her head. "Just a little tired."

"Okay. Ready to start the exams?"

"Um." She ducked her head out and looked up and down the hall. No Sabina. "Can you finish feeding? I just have something to discuss with Sabina. Do you know where she is?"

"Sure thing," he said, pouring more cat food into the bowls. "I think she went out back."

Audrey slowly meandered down the hallway, not sure how she was going to broach the subject. *Did you murder the veterinarian?* wasn't exactly the best way of going about it. But as she walked down the hall, more and more of the pieces seemed to fall into place. As a shelter manager, it was possible Sabina knew how to administer pentobarbital.

It was likely there was some on hand in the shelter, too, easily accessible.

That also meant that Sabina had the means.

When she reached the back of the clinic, she peered into the break room. No Sabina. She peeked into the storage room, too, but Sabina wasn't there. At the last door, the utility room, she heard Sabina cooing something in Italian, as if she was speaking to a baby.

Audrey pushed open the door to find Sabina with a large white-and-gold-striped cat. It was wearing a flowered scarf and a straw hat, and looked rather miserable. "Oh, Audrey! Tell Bella how pretty she looks! I just gave her her bath, and now she's ready for a night on the town!"

"You gave her a . . . a bath?" Audrey asked, tilting her head. Though Sabina was holding the poor creature down, Bella managed to get a paw loose and swipe the hat off her head. "Did she get into something? Because with her short coat, she really shouldn't need—"

"Oh, it's a service I do for all my favorite ladies," she said with a smile. "So that they look and smell nice for their men friends."

"That's very thoughtful of you," Audrey said as Sabina let go of Bella. Bella scampered off the counter as quick as can be, flying across the tub and sending water splashing on Sabina's face.

Sabina sighed as Bella attempted to bite the scarf off her neck. "Oh. Some of the girls are such *tomcats*." She giggled. "But Bella is so pretty, she just needs a little confidence!"

And Sabina was clearly a little off her rocker. She might have considered murder to be a fine solution to her problems. But did she have an alibi?

Audrey handed Sabina a towel. "How have things been going around here?"

Sabina wiped her face and shrugged. "I've been handling this place for twenty years. It's like clockwork now," she said. "I hope Vito hasn't been giving you any trouble?"

"Oh, no. Just the opposite. He's very sweet."

Sabina gazed at her doubtfully. "Well, that's good. I never could get through to that boy. He's a bit of a mystery to me. The younger age, you know? Attached to their phones and their crazy music and sulking all the time. Sometimes I think I could just kill him!"

Audrey smiled through gritted teeth. "Ha. But he's okay. I think he's a great kid. He has a big heart."

"Good. That is nice to hear. I try to raise a good boy, but there is much he never tells me. And you never can tell." She nodded.

"Sometimes I think he's on the right track. And sometimes I think he's headed the way of the heartless Dr. Mauro. I know you're not to speak ill of the dead, but some people make that so hard."

Audrey was glad Sabina brought that up, because she'd been trying to figure out how to do it herself. "So you heard about Dr. Mauro?"

She laughed. "Yes. Serves him right that someone finally did away with him."

"Yes. Did you hear how he died? Someone killed him with pentobarbital," she said casually, leaning against the examination table. "Isn't that interesting?"

Sabina let out a short "Ha!" and went to clean up the counter. "I'd say it serves him right for suggesting what he did at that last council meeting. It was absolutely barbaric, that he would even bring up such a thing."

"You mean, euthanizing all the stray pets?"

"Right! That's what he wanted to do!" the old woman said, throwing up her hands and raising her eyes to the ceiling. "Unbelievable, and unbelievably cruel and vile. He wanted to come into my place with a vial of that murder juice for each one of my strays. I told him he could stick that vial where the sun doesn't shine!"

"So you were at that meeting?"

"Oh yes, I was. Of course I was," she said, her voice hard with determination. "Anything I could do to get that man to back off my animals. I was the first one there, and I spoke out against him and everything. And then I confronted him on the front steps of the place. We almost got into a fist fight, him and me. I would've flattened him to the ground, the *idiota*. I think his death was the best thing that's ever happened to Lipari!"

"Wow," Audrey said. And here, when Audrey first asked about him at Pietro's, she hadn't seemed nearly as rabid in her hate for Dr. Mauro. But now, Sabina was almost frothing at the mouth. "You really didn't like him, did you?"

"No. I did not. But I wasn't the only one. And I was not as bad as some people. In fact, there is a whole group of people who hate the man. For one, there is Vittoria Vittelo, and her whole group."

"Vittoria . . . who?"

"Vittelo. Oh, she's a very sweet lady, but a bulldog, you know?" Sabina slapped her knee. "You get her riled up and she goes after you, no stopping! She's the president of the local animal welfare league. It's not much now, but she's trying to grow it. And she was there, outside, holding up signs against the doctor. She spit in his face!"

"She did?"

"Oh, yes. It was in our local paper. It was quite the story. She got arrested for it!" Sabina's fists clenched and unclenched. "I say, good for her!"

"When was this? She's not still in jail, is she?"

"Oh, no. She was out in a day. Bailed out by her people. She lives down by the sea, though I don't think she has an actual address. Her home is the whole island. You'll always find her out there, trying to get the tourists to stop feeding bread to the birds and things like that. She's the one holding a sign and screaming about the injustices of the world. She has a million crusades going on at once, all involving the animals she loves and the planet." Sabina smiled with admiration. "Quite a woman."

"Interesting," Audrey said, making a mental note of the woman's name. "Sabina . . . yesterday afternoon, when I was catching animals, what did you and Vito do?"

She smiled. "Yesterday . . . afternoon? Oh, I was with Vito the whole time. We were cleaning up the yard. Quite a lot of work to get all of that poop thrown away!"

"Oh. Yes," Audrey said, relieved. Vito would be able to confirm that. And so, unless they were both lying, it meant that she could strike two possible suspects off her list.

Only 1,994 more to go. Starting with this Vittoria Vittelo.

Because any woman crazy enough to spit in someone's face over something they were passionate about was probably brazen enough to commit murder over it, too.

*

There was still a lot of work to be done at the clinic, so as helpful as Vito had been to her, Audrey slipped quietly out just before closing time. The kid already had a few strikes against him. She didn't want him to follow her around and risk getting in trouble again.

The walk to town was downhill, so it wasn't a difficult one, and from going back and forth the past few days, Audrey already knew her way around the winding streets. At the end of the block, she turned toward the harbor and the rocky beach, to see a small collection of people gathered there. A woman was shouting something in Italian into

90

a bullhorn, about *tartarughe*, as she passionately stalked the beach, attempting to rouse up the crowd like a general would an army of soldiers.

Unfortunately, no one seemed very interested. There was a family of tourists on beach towels there with two small children who kept snapping pictures as if she was a famous attraction, and a few sulky teenagers were smoking cigarettes and mimicking her.

I wonder what that is all about, she thought, quickly putting the word *tartarughe* into her Google translate. *Turtles.*

Ah. Save the turtles.

Audrey kicked off her shoes and sunk her toes into the sand. It was cool, now that the sun was setting. The beach was nice, the waves calm, dappled with orange rays of the dying sun, and Audrey thought for a moment how she'd have loved to sit out here and just relax, maybe read a book. *If I ever have the time while I'm here, which face it—isn't going to happen.*

She snorted at the thought, then a little voice said, *If you accepted Gallo's offer to be Lipari's veterinarian, you would have the time. You could come here after work, every day, and unwind.*

She sighed and looked down at Nick, next to her. Even he seemed to enjoy frolicking in this new world. He was digging in the stony, volcanic sand, letting his tail sweep across it, making footprints in it. *He wouldn't mind, that's for sure.*

As she got closer, she saw the sign the woman was holding. It had a picture of a turtle on it. The woman had long, flowing gray hair, streaked with white, and was wearing an amorphous, flowing tunic and skirt that reached her toes. She screamed and shook her fist, pausing for effect, and Audrey had to believe that she was a great speaker, even though Audrey had no idea what she was saying. A few admirers applauded and gazed at her with awe, but as Audrey approached, some people peeled off and headed away, laughing, muttering, *pazza.*

That was one word Audrey knew. It meant *crazy lady.*

Finally, she finished her speech, and the random applause quickly dissolved. The woman put down her sign and sighed. Audrey stepped forward. "Vittoria Vittelo?"

The woman's eyes narrowed. "*Si?*"

"*Buonasera,*" Audrey said unsurely, wishing she had Vito to help her. "Um . . . *sapevate Dottore Mauro?*"

She frowned. "*Cretino. Perché lo chiedi?*"

Audrey stared. "Um . . ." She laughed. "Sorry. I don't know what that means. You don't speak English, do you?"

"I do," she said, her voice a low, no-nonsense rasp. She grabbed her signs and her sandals, and began to trudge toward the street. "I was asking why you ask about such a low, bad man. Terrible scum, he is."

"Oh, thank goodness you speak English," Audrey said. "I suppose you already heard what happened to him?"

"Of course I heard. Nothing escapes my ears, especially in a town as small as this," she said. "I've been living here in Lipari all my life. That's fifty years. I was born here. I know everything and everyone. I even know you."

Audrey blinked. "You do?"

She nodded and swept her long hair back behind her shoulders. There were long scraggles of black seaweed in there. Maybe she *did* sleep on the beach? "Yes. You arrive here on the ferry a couple days ago. I watch. I see. I see Matteo Gallo come and meet you at the pier, and that says to me, you are someone important, no?" She stroked her chin. In the dying sunlight, Audrey could see a few black whiskers there, sprouting from an unfortunate, dark wart at the very tip of it.

As they approached the street, a striped yellow cat came up to Vittoria. She reached down, petted it, and then pulled a handful of what looked like dry cat food from the pocket of her flowing skirt, feeding it to the kitty. "There you go, Luna," she said. "Good girl."

Then she straightened, and almost looked surprised that Audrey was still standing there. Audrey got the feeling that most people tried to steer clear of her, or didn't stay in her company for long. Audrey understood. Even in the fresh air, the woman smelled heavily of incense and body odor—sweet, and yet a bit putrid.

The kitty ran off, and Vittoria continued. "I see you around with that Sabina's boy, that handful, Vito. That tell me you know Sabina. And I hear through the grapevine there was a big fight between a new, young veterinarian and the old *cretino* . . ." She grinned widely, revealing yellow, crooked teeth. "Something tells me that you are that new veterinarian?"

Audrey nodded, astonished. Wow, either word really did get around fast, or this woman was extremely nosy. Or both. "That's right. That's pretty impressive."

"Ah." Vittoria waved the notion away and headed to a bench across the sidewalk from the beach. She set down her sign and began to wipe the sand from her feet. "You live here long enough, you hear all, notice all."

That was promising. "So you didn't like Dr. Mauro?"

She snorted. "That is like asking if I like the devil."

"Oh," Audrey said, trying to choose her words carefully. The last thing she wanted was a woman who'd spit in her enemy's face on her bad side. "Do you have any idea who could've killed him?"

"No. But I wish I knew who did it. I'd like to pin a medal on his chest. The man was no good. Very bad man," she said, plopping down on the bench and shaking her head as she gazed out at the shoreline. "Why you fight with him?"

"I didn't want to. I'm here to help control the stray pet population. All I wanted to do was give him some advice, speak to him, vet to vet, but he accused me of moving in on his business. That's *not* what I was trying to do. I have my own clinic in Mussomeli."

Vittoria nodded. "I believe you. He's a big *idiota*. He don't let no one tell him his business."

Audrey sat next to her. "I heard that you saw him at a council meeting and . . . had words, too?"

She laughed, with a glint of pride in her eyes. "I spit in his stupid face."

"Yes. That's what I heard. Why did you do that?"

Her laughter grew. "Oh, I had many, many reasons. The latest was that he was a murderer. He called it euthanasia, and I call it murder. Wiping out the stray pet population by poisoning their food supply was not humane. Not to mention that it would have murdered countless other wild animals. It was cruel. Too cruel. He was not a doctor. He was supposed to save lives, not destroy them."

Audrey nodded. "That is what I heard."

"You're no better. You put those kitties in jails. They no want to be in prison. They did nothing wrong."

"Well, they're suffering because there's not enough to eat. There's too many of them. I hoped to control the cat population by neutering the male animals. But he didn't seem to want to listen to outside ideas."

"That's right." She huffed. "I can tell you one thing. I am not sad he's dead. Typical sexist man. Big ego. Thought he knew everything. He would not let any woman tell him his business. I heard his office was a horror show. All the people who go in say it's not a good place. Dirty. Falling apart. Old equipment. He was too set in his ways to change anything."

"So you've never been inside his clinic?" Audrey asked. "Do you have any pets?"

She smiled. "All the animals in Lipari are mine. The ones in the sea, the ones on land, the ones in the air. I care for them all. To me, a house, four walls, is a jail. The world is my home, and the home of all creatures. And one of the ways I take care of the animals in this island is by not taking them to see that butcher." She leaned in, as if imparting a secret. "I can see you are not like him. You care for the Earth's creatures, even if you want to put them in prisons."

"Not forever. Just until they're neutered. That way they won't reproduce."

She smiled. "You're a good one. I like you."

"*Signorina Vittelo*," Audrey said, relieved to have gotten on her good side. It emboldened her enough to ask the next question. "You seem to be the eyes and ears of this island. Did you see anything suspicious last night, around dinner time, when Mauro was murdered?"

She went to a nearby trashcan, and to Audrey's horror, began to pick through it. She found a red child's sand bucket with a broken handle and placed it in her big shoulder bag. "No. I wish I'd been around. But only because I would've cheered the killer on!" She laughed harder, but this time, it dissolved into a phlegmy, wet cough. "No. I was at the harbor the whole evening, organizing a protest against the *idiota* tourists."

"Tourists?"

"Yes. They come here in droves, to fish our waters, and they're destroying the habitat of the creatures in the sea. The turtles! The poor turtles."

Oh. So that means not only did she not see anything, she can't be the killer. There were probably dozens of people who saw her on the harbor, if she organized the event.

"Well, thank you," Audrey said, turning toward the street. "I appreciate your—"

She froze.

Oh no. Here comes trouble.

94

CHAPTER EIGHTEEN

Heading Audrey's way, with one of the other police officers on her tail, was Officer Lorenzo.

She stiffened as she watched the two officers rapidly approaching her. From the look in Lorenzo's eyes, she wasn't happy.

Quickly, Audrey said, loudly enough that anyone nearby could hear, "So, Signorina Vittelo, where do you normally see the most strays on this beach?"

Vittoria gave her a confused look as the two officers stepped onto the sidewalk. Officer Lorenzo motioned to Audrey. "Can I speak to you, Miss Smart?"

She crossed her arms tightly in front of herself. "Uh. Sure. Of course. What can I do for you?"

The officer motioned her forward. "Privately?" Then she looked at Vittoria. "Don't go anywhere, Vittoria. We need to have a word with you, too."

Vittoria rolled her eyes. "As usual."

There was definite familiarity in their banter, as if they were old friends, or probably more accurately, old rivals. Audrey followed the older female officer down the sidewalk, until they were a safe distance away. The woman sighed. "What are you doing here?"

Audrey shrugged. "I was appointed by the council to solve the stray problem. I was just trying to get local opinion as to where the biggest stray population is usually found. I heard Ms. Vittelo is the person to ask."

Lorenzo gave her a doubtful look. "Right."

"It's true." At least, partly. "But you're wasting your time if you're interviewing Vittoria about the murder. She was at a protest last night at the harbor. At least, that's what she told me."

"We know that already. Remember what I told you, Miss Smart," she said, seeming to emphasize the word "Miss," just to get under Audrey's skin. "We don't need anyone meddling in this case. We have enough work to sort through on our own, without you adding any more to it."

"I'm not trying to add trouble. I was only trying to—"

"Whatever you were doing, whether you try to our not, is causing trouble. It's best if you stay in your lane, stick to your job, and leave the investigation to us."

Officer Lorenzo had to have been a mother, because after that stern tongue-lashing, Audrey felt a lot like the child found with her hand in the cookie jar. She nodded and started to back away.

"But, since you're here, I will fill you in on an interesting development," she said with a sly smile.

Audrey bristled. If the officer did want Audrey out of the investigation, giving her news of "interesting developments" was probably not the way to do it. Unless . . . unless there was something else up the officer's sleeve.

A chill went up Audrey's spine as a terrible thought came to her. Maybe they had discovered someone had broken into Mauro's office. Maybe the vet had a hidden camera somewhere in his office, or a witness had seen her climbing in the window.

She stiffened as she realized that she had a few of the stolen files in her bag. All it would take would be one search, and she'd be in some *big* trouble.

She pulled her purse closer to her side. "Oh? What would that be?"

"There were no fingerprints on the syringe. Not a single one, not even Mauro's," she noted lightly. "But there was a fine powder found, indicating that the killer had likely worn latex gloves. So that's really going against that suicide theory of yours, don't you think?"

Audrey's heart quickened. "I suppose it is."

"And the latex gloves are concerning. Where did they come from?"

Audrey's breath caught as she thought of the box of gloves in the back of Vito's car. But many people used latex gloves. It wasn't strange, considering the profession. Dr. Mauro probably used them all the time. She opened her mouth to say that, but Lorenzo beat her to it.

"Interestingly enough, Dr. Mauro was allergic to latex, and didn't use them at all in his practice," she said, making all the air leave Audrey's lungs in a rush. "So the killer must've brought them along with her."

Her. There could be no mistaking the officer's intention.

"Oh?" Audrey asked, nonchalant.

"Yes. Interesting, don't you think?" she said, her eyes carefully trained on Audrey.

She's trying to get me to give something away, she thought. But Audrey shook her head, trying to keep her reaction as normal as possible. "Not really. Latex allergies are common."

"Are they? Are *you* allergic?"

"No," she said. "In fact, I carry a package of latex gloves in my medical case. But a lot of people do. They're used at Sabina's shelter. They're used everywhere. And if the killer brought *his* own gloves with him, it tells me that it was planned ahead of time."

The officer considered this. "Yes, I suppose it does."

"Whoever went there, went there with the sole purpose of killing him," Audrey continued. "And like I said, I went there to talk reason into him. I didn't bring my medical bag, and I wasn't wearing gloves. I'm sure you found my prints everywhere. Wouldn't I have tried to conceal them, if I were the killer? And I certainly wouldn't have reported the crime if I was guilty of it."

She felt triumphant, repeating the words Gallo had said to her.

But Officer Lorenzo didn't seem convinced. She just said, "Hmm," and then started to walk past Audrey, toward Vittoria. She only got a few steps before turning. "Remember, Miss Smart. Don't go anywhere."

Audrey groaned and muttered under her breath, "Doctor."

Of course she wasn't going to go anywhere. The island was small, and now she got the feeling that the Lipari police were keeping a very close eye on her. As Officer Lorenzo quietly questioned Vittoria, she kept looking up, every so often, at Audrey. The other officer, too, seemed to be watching her every move. Were they following her?

Her stomach rumbled. She hadn't eaten all day. She grabbed her phone, looking for the nearest café to get something to eat, when she noticed a text. It was from Mason:

Hey, went by your house and your office and the girl there said you were gone for a few days. When you get back, can we talk?

A little thrill spiked in her, followed by dread. He'd probably tell her how he'd made up with his girlfriend, or some half-hearted excuse for leading her on, and "Sorry it didn't work out." The last thing she wanted to do was listen to that. Not that she had to worry about that anytime soon. She was stuck here in Lipari. Actually, compared to that conversation, a prison in Lipari didn't sound all that bad.

She started to type a message in return, and stopped. Her mind cycled through a dozen different replies, from "Get lost, loser" to "I'd love to." In the end, she decided not to respond at all.

Yes, that was better. Let him dangle a little, just like she'd been doing.

Pocketing her phone, she turned toward town, clutching her bag for dear life. Why had she let Vito talk her into breaking into the office? Now she had evidence on her person that tied her to the crime. And that wasn't good.

But maybe they'd decide she was the killer anyway . . . even without the evidence. Especially if they came up with no other leads.

She turned back toward the officer who was interviewing Vittoria, but gazing suspiciously at Audrey.

Definitely not good. Audrey really needed to find answers before they finished their investigation and decided that all signs pointed to her.

But first, an early dinner. Away from the prying eyes of Officer Lorenzo, she'd figure out who to talk to next.

CHAPTER NINETEEN

Audrey decided to stop at that outdoor café on the harbor that she'd noticed when the ferry first arrived on the shores of Lipari. It was on a wooden pier, hanging over the sea, and all the tables had red and green beach umbrellas, tilting different ways to shield against the bright sun. She got a table in the corner, closest to the ocean, and ordered a San Pellegrino and a Calabria panini, with salami, pepper-jack cheese, and pesto. There, the only thing to break her concentration would be the occasional cry of a child down by the seashore, or the squawk of a seagull, overhead.

She needed to concentrate now. She needed to think about just who she should interview next. It *was* good that Officer Lorenzo was thinking to interview the town busybody, especially considering Vittelo didn't like Mauro and had made such a scene at the council meeting. Audrey had to give the Lipari police force props for that. But since Vittoria Vitello was also the eyes and the ears of the town, Audrey got the feeling that they were interviewing Vittelo, not as a suspect, but as a potential witness.

Sipping her drink while she waited for the food to arrive, she shivered in the shade and the sea breeze. Her bare arms were slightly sunburned from her earlier foray to the beach. *And I didn't even get a chance to chill out and read a book,* she thought a little sourly.

The restaurant was busy, but it seemed to be mostly tourists. She scanned the area, half-expecting one of the Lipari police to be watching. But nobody was paying attention to her. She was in the corner, in a relatively secluded section of the pier, backed up to the ocean, so she carefully reached into her bag, leaving it on the bench beside her, and cracked open the next case file.

She didn't accomplish much. Every time someone came by, she quickly slammed the file closed, afraid that someone would see her with the stolen files. Even when the waiter came with her food, she jumped nearly sky high, expecting to see Officer Lorenzo, ready to snap handcuffs on her.

There has to be something here, she thought, taking a bite of her sandwich. The gooey melted cheese stretched out, clinging to her chin, but she wiped it hastily away. She got so involved in the research that before long, she went to grab her sandwich and realized she'd eaten the whole thing without even stopping to enjoy it. Had it tasted good? She swallowed, but couldn't remember.

Oh, but your hips will remember. It'll probably add another pound to your waistline, at least, Audrey thought as she pushed the plate away and continued to turn the pages.

She paused as she found something slipped haphazardly into one of the files. It was in Italian, but she quickly translated in her head. It was a third notice, dated only a couple months before, saying that the vet was required to cease operations until he took the proper steps to reinstate his license. So the doctor had been operating under an expired license? And his receptionist, whoever that was, hadn't attempted to renew it? Perhaps they'd forgotten . . . or had he had it revoked for some reason?

That was serious business. If he was ever found out, the fines would be enormous, and it could be even worse—he could've gone to prison.

Whatever the reason was, it meant one thing: Dr. Mauro shouldn't have been practicing veterinary medicine on the island.

And yet he was. He'd been their only hope.

At that, Audrey thought about Gallo's offer. The poor animals of Lipari—and the people who cared for them—certainly deserved better. Audrey felt sure she could give them that. It wouldn't take very much. And Gallo definitely seemed willing to make her comfortable here, and support her efforts.

Not to mention that it would be nice to avoid Mason Legare . . . possibly forever. *Take that, Legare! I didn't need you anyway.* She could just imagine the look on his face when he learned she was never coming back, moving on to greener pastures.

As she was entertaining that thought, smiling a little, she looked up and saw a familiar face beyond the tables, at the host stand.

It was Sabina. Audrey quickly stuffed the files away and waved to her.

She spotted Audrey and said something to the host, who handed her a menu. Then she came forward, weaving around the tables, until she reached Audrey. "Ah! I see you've already eaten!"

"Yes, I have. It was very good." *I think.*

The woman struggled to pull her body behind the bench and plopped down, opening the menu. "Their paninis are delicious here," she said. "I asked Vito to come with me but he say he have too much work to do. I think you created a monster!"

Audrey frowned. That was a little suspicious. Yes, Vito was a good kid, but Audrey didn't know many teens who'd turn down food. She had to wonder if he'd gotten rid of Sabina simply so that he could do a little sleuthing of his own. "Is he back at the shelter?"

She nodded. "He said you'd probably gone out to try to round up more strays?"

"Oh, yes. He's right. That's what I've been doing."

Sabina laughed. "Haven't been very successful, eh?"

"What do you mean?" Audrey shifted uncomfortably on the bench.

Sabina shrugged and peeked under the table. "Well, if you're collecting strays, then, where are they?"

That was what she *should* have been doing. That was what Gallo was expecting her to do. It was what he was paying her for. But all she'd been doing was meandering about, trying to find out more about this murder. "Oh, I haven't been having much luck," she said, throwing up her hands. "They must all be avoiding me!"

Just as she said that, she watched a mangy cat meander underneath one of the nearby tables, after a scrap of food. Luckily, Sabina didn't notice. She said, "I suppose you have gotten a reputation among them?" with a little giggle.

"Yes. And running after cats works up an appetite, so I just stopped for something to eat." She reached for her purse. "But if you'll excuse me, I'll leave you here, in the best seat in the place, and get back to it!"

"Of course!" Sabina said with a smile, glancing down at her menu. "Good luck."

Audrey managed a smile as she slid out from behind the table. *Catching strays while I'm the main suspect in a murder investigation? I'm going to need it.*

As soon as she paid for her lunch and headed off the pier, Audrey noticed another couple of cats scampering across the road, toward a fenced-in lot with a broken-down building, its windows boarded up. Audrey watched them go inside and gritted her teeth. It was a perfect refuge for stray cats. She'd likely find a slew of them in there.

Nick met her on the sidewalk, and was already on high-alert, his ears perked up and his nose twitching.

"What do you say, bub? You think we should check it out?"

He raced off toward it, narrowly avoiding a couple on a bicycle-built-for-two lazily meandering down the road. He was clearly up for the adventure, disappearing through an invisible hole in the fence faster than her eyes could track him.

CHAPTER TWENTY

"Nick!" she called as she ran across the street, trying to figure out how he gained entrance. Now, she'd have to do the same thing—but she was nowhere near as small and spry as her pet.

She inspected the chain-link fence and found an opening in it that would allow her to pass through. She reached into her bag, found her gloves, and slipped them on. Then, taking a deep breath, she hurried across the street toward the old stone house and ducked through the gap in the fence.

She heard the sound of something inside, even before she reached the window. Somewhere, a cat let out a little shriek. Climbing over the rubble and debris scattered over the front lawn, she stepped up the crumbling front stoop and leaned over, craning to see through a place in the window where one of the wooden boards had been pulled back.

Blinking, she tried to adjust her eyes to the darkness. Several small forms moved within. The first things she saw were several sets of eyes, unblinking, staring back at her.

It was a destroyed living room that, funnily enough, didn't look much different from her own home in Mussomeli, with its tattered wallpaper, broken light fixtures, and pitted floors. The cats seemed to like it just fine, though. She started to count them, but lost count as they scampered away. There were at least a dozen cats calling this living room home.

Somewhere inside, Nick hissed.

"Great, making friends all over the place, are we, bub?" she mumbled, squinting to see better.

Audrey shoved aside the broken board with the heel of her hand, giving herself enough of a space to squeeze through. Climbing up onto the window ledge, she eased herself inside. Somehow, after her escapades earlier that day, slipping into the window of the vet office, this was a breeze. Her feet came down in a puff of dust on the ruined wood flooring. The dust was thick, but full of tiny little cat prints, heading all over the house. She sneezed as she looked around, spotting a young gray, on the decaying mantel of a stone fireplace. Nick was keeping him at bay. He let out a little mewl of concern as he tried to find a way down.

"Hello, baby," she said as its green eyes glinted. Looking around, she spied an overturned milk crate and waded through the debris to pick it up. *Well, I can't get in your whole family, but I might be able to catch just one of you. That's a little bit of progress.*

She grabbed the crate and lifted it up. Out spilled a pile of dirt and what looked like a dead rat. The strong scent of earth and something rotten rose up to meet her.

The panini in her stomach threatened to come back up her throat. She swallowed it back and took the crate over to the gray cat, who was watching her curiously, all the while licking its paws.

"All right, honey," she cooed to it, treading carefully toward it. "I'm not here to hurt you, I'm just going to take you in and get you looked at, all right?"

The cat simply watched her, unafraid, as she crept up and started to scoop him into her arms.

"That's right. No problem," she said, beginning to lift it off the mantel.

Suddenly it screeched and flew forward, claws extended. It caught her on the side of the face before jumping onto her shoulder, then gracefully hopping to the ground. She turned to grab ahold of it, but it was too quick. It slipped right through her fingers, and as she lunged for it, she lost her balance and fell to her knees. Choking in the thick layer of dust on the floor, she watched it scamper up the decaying staircase to the second floor.

Her cheek began to sting. She reached up and touched it, only to find her fingers dark with blood. *Fantastic. I've gotten about three million scratches on this island since I got here, and I've caught about . . . one stray cat. I'd say the cats are winning.*

The sun was just about gone, too, the room growing even darker by the second.

Whoa. It got dark really fast. What's going on out there?

Whatever it was, it was probably not a good idea to be in this abandoned place after dark, considering it was a hazard in the daytime, when she could see the potential dangers. So giving up, she went to the window and pushed aside the broken board. As she did, one of the cats came down the stairs. She knew she was only imagining it, but it seemed triumphant to be getting rid of her.

"I'll be back," she murmured, then turned and eased herself out the way she'd come.

When her feet hit the ground outside the condemned home, Nick was already outside, waiting for her. She looked up and saw that clouds had begun to gather, blocking out the sun on the horizon. The white bodies of the seagulls stood out among the multiplying black clouds. The wind was picking up, signaling a coming storm. "Let's get out of here, Nick," she murmured to him, "before we get drenched."

She shivered as her phone buzzed in her pocket. She pulled it out to find a call coming in from the clinic in Mussomeli. She brought it to her ear. "Hello?"

"Audrey? You didn't call today," a voice, sounding rather timid, said. It was Concetta, but she sounded a little perturbed.

"I know, I'm sorry. I've been busy. I was going to call, but it—" *It completely slipped my mind.* "Is everything okay?"

"Well, it *was*," she said, her voice shaking a little. "Up until about an hour ago. Someone just brought in a stray dog, and I think . . . well, it has all the classic signs of rabies."

"Rabies? Are you sure?"

"No. I don't know for sure. But it was acting really crazy. At first I thought that it just didn't want to be restrained. But then it bit me. And after I cleaned up the mess, I noticed it was foaming a little at the mouth."

Oh, no. "Okay, Concetta. Listen to me. You know where I keep the pentobarbital, right?"

"Yes."

"The first thing you need to do . . . is put the dog down."

She paused. "I know that, but I—"

"Concetta. You know I'm the last person who'd advocate for ending an animal's life. But rabies is untreatable. It's going to die anyway, and painfully, and it might infect other animals while it's at it. So the most humane thing you can—"

"Well, that's the problem. It escaped."

Audrey blinked. "It escaped?"

"Yes. I tried to go after it, but it disappeared. And now that bite . . . it's getting a little puffy." Concetta sounded far from the calm, controlled woman whose favorite refrain was, "I've got it under control!" Right now, she was clearly a little frantic, her voice far away, trembling. "And well, I haven't had the rabies vaccine, so I'm a little concerned . . ."

Audrey dragged a hand down her face. This was the last thing she needed, now, when she couldn't even leave the island. "Okay, Concetta. Listen to me. I want you to close the clinic. Right now. Call your doctor immediately and tell him that you think you may have been exposed to rabies. Do you understand?"

"Yes. I understand."

"All right. They'll know what to do. Don't worry about the clinic. I'll call someone to have them come in and take care of the animals there. You need to take care of yourself."

"But what about all the appointments you have?"

"I'll have that person cancel all the appointments for the next few days."

She sniffled, and Audrey realized the poor young woman was crying. "I'm so sorry, Audrey. I don't—"

"Please! It's not your fault. What's important is that you take care of your health."

"Are you coming back?"

She let out a slow breath. "I can't. I have a little emergency here myself, which makes it impossible for me to leave. But it's okay. Everything will be fine. Now go and call your doctor."

Quickly, she dialed the number for Councilman Falco. The phone rang several times before going to voicemail. *"Hai raggiunto l'ufficio del Consigliere Falco . . ."* When she heard the beep, she said, "Councilman, it's Audrey Smart. Please call me when you get this message. Thanks."

She hung up. That wasn't good enough. She needed to get in touch with someone *now*.

Quickly, she dialed G at La Mela Verde, but hung up when a woman answered, sounding annoyed and harried. It was the dinner rush, and his cafe was always hectic during the dinner rush. She couldn't saddle him with this.

Audrey hung up the phone and shivered. Everything seemed to be falling apart there, and there was very little she could do about it.

Don't even think about it. You can't.

But the more she tried to think of alternatives, the more certain she became. Her hands were completely tied. She had no other choice.

So she did the only thing she could think to do. She picked up her phone and placed another call. A moment later, a voice said, "Hello?"

She let out a shuddery breath. "Mason?"

106

CHAPTER TWENTY ONE

"Yeah. That you, Boston?" Mason's gruff voice, with a bit of a Southern twang, came through. He sounded so far away, but even far away, that drawl of his made her heart flutter.

"Yes. It's me," she said, reminding herself to be aloof. *He broke your heart, remember? You need his help as a neighbor. That's all.*

"Hello! You get my text? I've been looking all over for you. That girl at your clinic said you went—"

"Yeah, I did," she said, cutting him off. "I'm here in Lipari on another assignment, working with the strays here. And there's a big problem in Mussomeli. I need you to do a big favor for me."

"Sure. Name it."

She let out a little sigh of relief. That was one thing about Mason. He may have broken her heart, but he was dependable, and always willing to help her out in a jam. And she'd had many of those since moving to Sicily. "Thank you. Okay. A stray dog was brought into the clinic and it bit Concetta. She thinks it might have had rabies."

"Rabies? Yeah? That ain't good."

"She hasn't been vaccinated. So I told her to close the clinic and get to her doctor. But I need you to do a few things for me. You might want to write this down."

"That's all right. I got it."

"You sure?"

"My mind's a steel trap."

She wasn't so sure about that, because he did have a bit of an ego on him, but she wasn't in the mood to argue with him. "All right. First, call Falco on the council and tell him that there's a stray dog in town possibly infected by rabies. They should keep a lookout for any animal acting strange. Please tell Falco that I will be there as soon as I can, but at the moment, I'm held up."

"Held up? Everything okay, Boston? You don't sound good. I hope you're not getting yourself in any trouble."

"Yeah. I mean, no. No trouble at all!" She tried to sound nonchalant, but it didn't work. Her voice had an obvious tremor. "I'm fine. But I can't talk about it now. Also, I need you to go into the clinic and take care of the animals there. Just as you have before." She knew he could handle that. He'd done it before. "If any of them seem to be acting violent, or strange, or foaming at the mouth, do not go near it. Call me immediately."

"All right. I've got it."

"And then I need you to go through my appointment book and cancel any appointments for the rest of the week. Call them and tell them I've had an emergency, and I'll be in touch to reschedule."

"Consider it done."

"And call me. Please. I feel terrible I can't be there."

"Don't worry, Boston. I'll take care of it."

She sighed with relief. Despite what had happened, she still trusted him, probably more than anyone else in this country. "That's it. Thanks, Mason."

"Okay. Call the council, take care of the animals. I'm on it," he said, in that confident drawl of his. Then there was a pause. "Audrey, I came looking for you because I wanted to talk to you about—"

"Mason," she blurted, cutting him off. She didn't want to go into this. Not now. Not when everything was falling apart. "I can't talk. I'm sorry. Just—call me as soon as you hear anything."

She quickly ended the call and threw her head back, staring up at the darkening sky. The clinic in Mussomeli would be closed, the stray population was in jeopardy, and the people in town were in jeopardy, too. This was the last thing she needed to worry about now, in the midst of a murder investigation in which she was the prime suspect. Could there be anything else piled up on top of her list of worries?

As if someone above had heard her, loud thunder crashed above, and lightning slit the sky. Then the heavens opened up, and it began to pour.

Nick whimpered and rushed between her legs for cover, but when that didn't work, he scampered off, into a crack between two buildings. "Fair-weather friend!" she shouted after him.

She held her purse over her head and tried her best to dodge raindrops as she rushed for cover, but even so, by the time she reached the opening in the fence, she was already drenched. *Time to go back to the shelter,* she said, hugging herself. *Maybe I can find some answers there, since I haven't been able to find anything in town all day.*

As she walked, rain dripped off the edge of her nose. Using her purse as an umbrella was clearly not working, so she let it fall. But as she went to hoist it onto her shoulder, the fabric of it gave way, and the contents of the purse spilled to the ground. Everything—her wallet, her phone, and all the folders she'd stolen—landed in a puddle of muddy water.

"No!" she cried, stooping to collect it all.

She shoved the items into her ruined purse, scooping up handfuls of mud at the same time. Once she had it all, she hugged it to herself, trying in vain to keep it all dry. She ducked under the overhang of a building and inspected the papers. They were a wet, muddy mess, sticking together.

"Great," she muttered.

Not that it mattered much if the files got ruined. There wasn't anything that was very helpful in them. All of that risk, all of that work obtaining them, and they hadn't been worth much at all. It seemed like there was absolutely nothing in them of any value.

She stared at the papers, trying to get them in some semblance of order. This was what she needed an assistant for. She regretted not bringing Vito with her. The results wouldn't have been any worse than what she'd come up with alone. Sometimes she was just too stubborn to admit defeat. That was one thing she'd had trouble coming to grips with—she couldn't do everything herself. No one could. At her practice in Boston, there'd been a team, so that if one of the vets had to go away, someone could always fill in.

Here was no different. She needed people. People like Vito, and Mason, and Concetta . . .

Suddenly, a question popped into her head.

Dr. Mauro had a practice catering to all the animals on the island. Did he have any help managing that practice?

He'd had a receptionist's desk, but Audrey hadn't seen any clue in that front office area to say who it had been. Not that she'd looked very closely; at the time, she'd been too worried about getting caught. Perhaps it was a vet tech. Dr. Mauro had been getting on in age. Was it possible he'd done all his work alone? Even the best veterinarians needed some help, and from what she'd heard, Dr. Mauro had left a lot to be desired.

Wiping the rainwater from the tip of her nose, she dove into the messy files in her arms, gently turning the damp pages as best she could, since they were fragile and sticking together. The words blurred, and in the descending darkness, it wasn't easy to make out the print. She squinted. Atop one, she saw a name she'd never seen before: *Flora Abruzzo.* It looked like the report had been prepared by this person.

Flora Abruzzo. Maybe all the work put into obtaining the files would be worth it, after all. It could be a lead. She'd have to ask Sabina or Vito and find out if they knew the woman.

It was getting darker, but the rain was starting to slow. Unfortunately, she was soaked and exhausted, and though the walk to the shelter was only about a mile, it'd be an uphill journey. *Just like everything I've been doing lately.*

Just then, lightning flashed across the clouded sky and thunder rumbled, shaking her. Taking a deep breath, she'd just made the decision to head out when someone suddenly stepped out from the alley and blocked her path.

CHAPTER TWENTY TWO

Audrey let out a startled gasp as a man stepped in front of her. He looked a bit like a koala, with a pushed-down nose and two tufts of gray hair at his ears. At first, Audrey thought he was going to ask her for her wallet—that's what would have happened if she'd been caught in an alley in Boston. But as the man kept speaking in mile-a-minute Italian, Audrey eventually made out the word *furetto* and determined he was talking about some kind of animal.

"Slow down, please," she begged as the man motioned behind him. "You say you have an animal? Injured?"

"Emergenza!" the man shouted, frantic. *"Emergenza!"*

"Oh. Emergency? Okay, please. Lead the way."

Stuffing her broken bag under her arm, she quickly followed the man down the alley and up the street, not even bothering to dodge puddles now, since she was soaked to the skin. All the while she had to wonder how this man knew who she was. It wasn't like she was wearing a sign that said *Veterinarian.* But word clearly traveled fast around here, which was why just about everyone knew of Mauro's death.

And how fortunate that she'd been passing this way, just when he was having an emergency with his pet! As Audrey struggled to keep up, the hairs on the back of her neck stood at attention. It was Mason's voice that she heard then: *Audrey. You don't know this man. This could be a ploy to get you alone so that he can hurt you. You need to be more careful.*

Yes, she often barged into situations head-first, without thinking. How many times had she had close calls in Mussomeli? Mason was her voice of reason and had helped her out of quite a few scrapes. Even now, he was helping her. As much as she wanted it not to, her heart hurt with the thought of him. She couldn't deny it. She missed him.

The rainstorm had just about ended, and even a little bit of sun began to poke through the clouds, by the time the man stopped in front of a rusted screen door. He paused for a moment and looked back solemnly, as if to warn her about something. Then he opened up the door and let her pass through into a living room.

Her sneakers made a *squick-squick-squick* noise as she stepped inside. She looked down at the tiny puddle she was creating on the cement floor. "Is this—?"

"Non ti preoccupare," he said dismissively, ushering her through. *"Sbrigati!"* Hurry up!

The room was small and austere, the only decoration on the white stucco wall a wooden cross. Beneath it, there were at least a dozen people, men, women, and children, all standing around the animal as if paying last respects to a beloved family member at a funeral. Their faces were grim, and a few of them were crying.

Audrey had seen devoted pet owners, and loved whenever people treated pets as family, but she'd never seen such utter desolation in a room. The man shouted at them in Italian to move aside, and they did. With all the drama, she thought she'd see a child lying there, near death.

Instead, taking up a tiny bit of space on a white pillow at the head of the bed, covered in lace-edged sheets, was a tiny ferret. Its black eyes stared miserably at nothing.

"Oh. A . . . ferret?" She looked around, sure that there was some mistake.

But then a woman leaned forward and kissed its tiny paw. As she moved close, a tear dropped onto the pillow beside the creature, darkening the fabric.

Well . . . who am I to judge? I have a fox as a pet, and I'd probably be devastated if something happened to him.

"What seems to be the problem?" Audrey asked, kneeling beside it.

A few of the people began to speak in Italian, but a young girl in braids, who was probably the same age as Vito, said, "Milo is very bad. We found him this morning. He'd chewed through a lamp cord and we think he electrocuted himself."

Sure enough, the animal's fur around his mouth appeared to be a little singed. Audrey placed her bag on the ground and pulled out her stethoscope. She checked his heart rate, which was a bit elevated, and turned him over, then pried open the animal's mouth. Sure enough, he had the tell-tale black mark over his tongue that indicated electrocution.

"Poor thing," she said as the rest of the crowd looked over her, silent as a grave. "Was he out for a long time?"

The girl shrugged. "We don't know. When we found him, he was awake and acting strange, and then we found the chewed-up cord."

"Has he had any seizures?"

The girl shook her head.

"Well, his heart seems good and I don't hear any fluid in the lungs, so there's a good chance it isn't anything too serious and he will be just fine. Still, he has a burn on his tongue so he's probably going to be reluctant to eat anything soon. If he starts to have trouble breathing, I want you to find me right away." She grabbed her prescription pad, which was a little damp, and a pen, and started to write out a prescription. "I want you to get these filled. This is an antibiotic for his mouth and a diuretic which should help keep everything clear. All right?"

The girl took the slip of paper and nodded. "Yes. Thank you!" She turned to the crowd and started to translate. Everyone in the crowd sighed with relief, and began to gather around Audrey, hugging and kissing her cheeks.

"No, oh, no problem at all," she said, gathering up her things. The koala man thrust a few bills into her hand, but she quickly handed it back. "Oh, no. No charge. It's fine."

An older woman spoke to her in an almost argumentative tone, and handed her a few jars of what looked like pasta sauce. Audrey looked at the young girl, who shrugged. "Mama insists that you take that. And she doesn't take no for an answer."

"All right. Thank you. Please. I'm at Hotel Lipari if you need anything!"

The young girl grabbed Audrey's hand and succeeded in keeping the rest of the family at bay so that she could guide Audrey outside. When they were out there, she closed the door and sighed. "Sorry," she said with a smile. She whirled a finger near her head. "My family is a little *pazzo*."

"Oh, no. That's fine! That's what I'm here for!" Audrey said, wiping the water dripping from her hairline away from her eyes. "Really, it's no trouble . . . I'm sorry, what's your name?"

"Amalia." She eyed Audrey with concern. "Can I get you a towel?"

"Oh, it's fine. I'm probably going to stop by the hotel and change anyway. I got a little held up trying to rescue a few strays from that old house on the corner."

The girl smiled, baring pretty white teeth. "Oh, yes, that house has been like that for ages. Since I was a kid. I told Dr. Mauro about it, thought he might do something, but no."

"So he knew about it?"

The rainstorm had passed, and now the stars were popping out everywhere in the clear, dusky-blue sky. The warm air was starting to dry Audrey's clothes, leaving them stiff and uncomfortable. They began to walk together up the street. "Oh, yes. In his defense, though, he had a lot on his mind. There are a lot of strays around here." She sighed. "Very terrible, what happened to him. I'm sure you heard?"

Audrey nodded. "It was terrible. So he was Milo's vet?"

"Yes. That's right. Ever since we got him. He took good care of him. Which was why, when he was hurt, Papa didn't know what to do. Thank goodness I saw you, and knew who you were. So I told Papa, and he ran out and waved you down."

Audrey raised an eyebrow. "So you thought Dr. Mauro was a good doctor?"

"Yes." She laughed. "Oh, obviously, you've heard all the rumors about him. And Mama and Papa would be the first to tell you they were all true. But he wasn't a bad man. He was a very good doctor for many years. My parents took all of our animals to him, even before I was born, and he took very good care of them all."

"I did hear rumors. That he was misdiagnosing pets, working under an expired license . . ."

Amalia nodded. "Yes. It's all true. A few years ago, he and his wife of like, thirty years separated. Papa said that really made him go off the deep end. That was the start. He couldn't cope with it. And so he let the practice slide. Everything began to fall apart. At first, he just missed a few appointments. But it only got worse and worse. He stopped caring for himself. The clinic went to pot. He said some animals were fine when they were not. He didn't seem to care about anything."

"He's going through a divorce?"

"Went. It was all over town. Very bitter. Their fights were so loud and terrible! Once, she actually tried to run him over with her car, in the middle of the street! Then she took all his clothes and belongings, hauled them out to the end of the pier, and tossed them over! They hated each other at the end." Her eyes gleamed with the excitement of the gossip. "I don't think he has been the same since. But who could blame him?"

A bitter divorce, Audrey thought. *That must've been the dirty laundry that Sabina was afraid to talk about.* "Where is the wife?"

Amalie shrugged. "I don't know. I guess she still lives in their house on *via Oliva.* Big white building on the hill. But if she does, she doesn't go out much. Dr. Mauro moved into the apartment over his clinic. I think he just wanted to get away from her in the end. He just wanted to be done with the confrontation."

"I met him once," Audrey said, thinking, *He didn't strike me as a person who didn't care. In fact, he cared too much that I was infringing on his business.* "And at that point he didn't seem averse to confrontation. In fact, I tried to speak to him about working on fixing the stray problem, and he shut me out."

Amalia giggled. "I heard."

"You did?"

"Of course! The whole town did. You had quite the audience, didn't you? That's how I knew you were in Lipari. That was an exciting bit of gossip—well, until Dr. Mauro was found dead."

"He seemed to care an awful lot about me stepping on his toes, then."

"Yes. I think it makes sense."

"It does?"

She nodded. "Dr. Mauro was a very proud man. As much as he might've been letting things with his business slide, this is where he grew up. He took a lot of pride in being important to us, our only veterinarian. So I can understand him feeling a little territorial about his practice and not wanting anyone to move in and change things, after working here forty years. It must've been hard for him."

They'd walked to the end of the block. Just then, a voice down the street, behind them, called, rather harshly, "Amalia!"

She stiffened. "Oops! Sorry! I've got to go. I was in the middle of chores when we found poor Milo. I need to clean the bathroom." She wrinkled her nose. "Take care, Doctor!"

"You, too. And please let me know how Milo is!" she called, as the girl rushed down the sidewalk, toward her home, braids flying out behind her.

Audrey took a few moments to look around, trying to orient herself in the intersection. She noticed the shoreline and the pier and then headed in that direction, hoping that was where her hotel was. Her clothes were now so stiff and tight, they were chafing her skin, and her underwear was wet, which wasn't the nicest feeling.

She took a step off the curb, thinking about what Amalia had said. *A bitter divorce. An ex-wife who nearly killed him. Living in a big white house on via Oliva.*

It was definitely worth looking into. But first, she really wanted to get out of these wet clothes, maybe get a hot bath, and *definitely* have a glass of wine. She needed it.

CHAPTER TWENTY THREE

Just got back from the clinic. Everything's fine. All appointments for this week are cancelled. Stop worrying your pretty little head, Boston.

Audrey smiled at the text from Mason. She was wearing a fluffy white robe from the hotel, enjoying a late room-service dinner of *antipasti* and Chianti, and relaxing after a nice, warm bath. A little luxury after the past two days was just what she needed. In her tipsiness after consuming two glasses of wine, she read Mason's text, imagining him saying the words in that sexy Southern drawl of his, and her body quivered.

Stop it, Audrey. Stay strong. She sighed, throwing herself back against the pillows on her bed.

Quickly, she typed in: *Did you call Falco?*

A moment later, he replied with: *I did you one better. I went over and saw him. He's putting the area on high alert about a possible case of rabies. He says not to worry.*

She smiled. That was good. *Thanks. Have you seen Concetta?*

His response was: *Yes. The doctor thinks the bite isn't too serious but he's started her with treatment.*

Well, that was good. Mason, her knight in shining armor. Saving the day for her, again. This time, though, she resisted any impulse to gush and responded with a curt: *Thank you.*

When you coming back, Boston?

Hmm. Sure, he was wondering that. Without her there, he couldn't get free medical advice for his Mastiff, Polpetto. Initially quite the reluctant dog owner, Mason usually had a question a day about his new pet.

She sent as short a reply as she could think of: *Not sure yet.*

Then, of course, he had to go and do the thing that would ensure he stayed on her mind for the rest of the night. He wrote: *Miss you.*

She stared at those words, her heart thrumming.

Then she quickly exited out of the message. *Get a grip, Audrey.* All his charming words weren't going to work on her. She was determined not to let him worm his way under her skin again, no matter how adorable he was. Been there, done that. It still stung, just as much as it had the day she arrived on his doorstep to see he had "company." *I'm done with that. If being away from Mason has proven anything, it's that we were just fine as we were. Friends. That's all.*

She picked up a bit of crusty Italian bread and dipped it in the oil from the salad, then tore off a bite. Savoring the taste of the fresh herbs, she looked at the television set. She kept it on at a low volume, just to keep her company, but it was tuned to some Italian soap opera. The moment she made the "Friends" determination in her head, the handsome male lead took the buxom brunette in his arms and kissed her passionately.

"Ugh," Audrey mumbled as she watched them tearing at each other's clothes. "Get a room."

Audrey, do you really need a reminder that love often ends up going bad? Look at what happened to Dr. Mauro. His wife nearly flattened him with his own car!

Which reminded her . . . after what Amalia had said after she saw to her pet ferret, she couldn't help but be intrigued about the ex–Mrs. Mauro.

She turned off the television and picked up her phone. Then she Googled *"Mauro Lipari divorce."*

A number of results came back that had nothing to do with Dr. Mauro. She scrolled through each one until she came to *Giacomo Alto, Esquire, Divorce Attorney, Lipari.* She translated the website, and from what she could tell, he was the only divorce attorney on the island.

If I was a betting person, I'd wager he probably knows something about the case, she thought, clicking on the phone number and placing the call.

Because it was after hours, she expected to get a voicemail recording. So she was surprised when a voice said, "Alto."

"Um . . . Mr. Alto?" She thought for sure she'd get a receptionist. But Lipari was a small island—how many divorces could they possibly have? "Is this Mr. Alto, the divorce attorney?"

"Si," a confused voice said, and then there was a pause. "Ah. Let me guess. Is this the American veterinarian?"

Now it was Audrey's turn to be confused. "Yes . . . how did you—"

"I figured you would be knocking on my door soon."

"You did?"

"Look. I'm about ready to leave for the night. But if you can get here in the next five minutes, I'll answer any questions you might have. My office is on *via Lido*, near the pier. Can't miss it."

Audrey sat up and looked at the clock. It was just after eight. She grabbed the towel off her head. "Yes. I can do that. Leaving right now," she said.

"See you then."

He hung up, and Audrey sprang into action. She tore off the robe and threw on some clothes, ran a brush haphazardly through her hair, and headed out the door in record time.

*

Audrey was still finger-combing knots out of her wet hair when arrived at the office building on *via Lido,* across from the pier. Nick scampered along behind her, curious because the last time she left him, she told him she was going in for the night. The building was a charming one, with bulbs made to look like candles flickering in the windows, and bright red shutters a contrast to the white stucco walls. An oval-shaped shingle sign hung from the door that said, *Giacomo Alto, Avvocato* in stately gold script. Though the place faced the harsh wind coming off the sea, it suffered from none of the neglect that Mauro's office had—the windows were clean, the front welcome mat was free of debris, and when Audrey went inside, the air smelled of fresh paint and pine-scented cleaner.

"Stay here, bub," she warned Nick, though he was already holding back, dutiful as ever.

Inside, the waiting room was spacious and well-appointed, with rich leather chairs, thick red carpeting, and painting depicting various seaside scenes. As she stepped into the empty room, a door in the back opened, and a bald man with dark, bushy eyebrows poked his head out. "Ah. Dottore Smart. Come this way."

She followed him into an office with several diplomas and photographs of the man with a yacht, or standing near an impressively large fish. The man was clearly a lover of the sea, judging from those and all the nautical décor. She sat down in one of two chairs next to a coffee table made from an old ship's wheel. "Sorry to bother you so late."

119

"No bother at all. I knew you were coming. I—" He stopped and peered at her, just underneath her chin. He pointed to his chest. "You missed . . ."

She looked down and realized she'd skipped a button and misaligned the buttons on her shirt. As she was buttoning, she realized she'd also forgotten to zip the fly on her shorts. She discretely pulled it up. "And how did you know that?"

"Well, after that row you had with my client."

Audrey stiffened. Did *everyone* know about that? "What do you mean?"

"Well, come now, in a town such as this, there are no secrets. When I learned of the doctor's death, I assumed they'd probably target you as the murderer." He leaned back in his chair and laced his hands together. "What surprises me is that the police haven't come to me yet."

"They haven't?"

"No. But everyone thinks you're the killer."

Audrey shifted uncomfortably on the leather chair so that it made a peculiar farting noise. "And what makes them think that? Just because I had an argument with him?"

"That, and because you're a stranger. We haven't had a murder in Lipari in decades, and then you show up, start arguing with a man, and suddenly, he's dead? It doesn't look good."

Yes, it doesn't, all admit that. But that's just my bad luck.

"Maybe. But from what I hear, Mrs. Mauro had quite a few of those with her husband, too. They were in the middle of a divorce, yes?"

"That's why I figured you'd be here, to ask me that." He smiled. "But unfortunately, I'm not at liberty to disclose the particulars of the case my client had pending."

Then why have me come all the way here? Something tells me that's just a formality. There's something he wants to tell me. I just need to ask the right questions.

"Even if the possibility exists that his wife could've murdered him?"

He shook his head. "Sorry. It's really impossible for me to say."

"But he's dead. Doesn't that change things? Technically, he's not your client anymore."

He nodded and leaned forward conspiratorially. "Well . . . between you and me, Doctor, I will let you know that divorce papers had been served to him. Not once. Not twice. Numerous times. If you understand what I mean."

Her eyes narrowed. "He didn't sign them? Why not?"

He pressed his lips together. Then he said, "That, I can't help you with."

She pushed away from his desk and stood up, thinking. If he was refusing to sign divorce papers, that could definitely be a reason for Mrs. Mauro to commit murder. *I need to talk to her.* "She still lives here, doesn't she? In their big white house on the hill?"

He nodded. "From what I can gather."

"What is her name?"

He stood up to escort her to the door. "Loretta Mauro. But again, you did not hear it from me, but the woman is absolutely crazy. No wonder she drove my client insane, so that he could barely function. She kept beating on him and beating on him until he lost his mind. But he was just a silly man, refusing to put the woman out of his life, insisting that they could patch things up. Poor man."

Outside, a cool mist was filtering in from the sea, blanketing everything in an eerie haze. Audrey looked back at him in the dim candlelight as he showed her to the door. "From what you're saying, it sounds like you think she's guilty?"

He shrugged. "If you'd done it, you wouldn't have come to me. You'd probably have left the island by now. And so if it's not her, who else would it be? The person who'd commit cold-blooded murder like that would have to be crazy, and she fits the bill. Not to mention that she had a motive."

Audrey nodded. That was exactly what she was thinking. "Thank you. I really appreciate your time."

He waved goodbye to her and went back in, leaving her alone near the pier in a rapidly descending fog. In the streetlights, the mist looked like ghostly fingers, reaching down to grab ahold of her. Shivering, she looked around the empty streets. Luckily, just then, Nick poked his head out from the buildings and stood on the sidewalk, waiting to escort her back to the hotel.

She smiled. "You're not afraid of anything, are you, big guy?"

He simply scampered ahead. Behind her, she heard the creak of a gate, an eerie, echoing sound, and picked up her pace. She couldn't wait to be back in her room.

Tomorrow, she'd visit that big white house on a hill, and try to speak with Dr. Mauro's crazy wife.

CHAPTER TWENTY FOUR

Early the next morning, Audrey poured herself a terrible cup of coffee from the in-room coffee service and hurried downstairs, looking at her phone's GPS and trying to determine where *via Oliva* was. When she located it, she headed out, walking away from the pier, up the hill, barely paying any attention to Nick, trailing at her heels.

Suddenly, a loud beep startled her. She lifted her nose from her phone just as she tripped over a crack in the sidewalk and nearly face-planted on the ground. She caught herself, but not before her coffee went flying and her knee hit the crumbling pavement.

"Whoa! Are you okay?" a voice said. It was Vito. He'd stopped the car in the middle of the narrow road and was rushing toward her, trying to help her up.

She rolled until she was sitting and looked at her bloody knee. Her coffee cup rolled off into the gutter, spilling its contents as it went.

"Fine," she muttered, annoyed, as she retrieved her phone. At least that wasn't broken. Nick crawled onto her lap, attempting to lick her wound, but she nudged him away. "You scared me."

"Sorry. Geez," he said, wincing as he looked at her knee. "Hold on."

He about-faced to head toward his car, probably to get the medical kit. But as he did, a car came up behind his and beeped. "Don't worry about it," she called to him. "I'll meet you at the shelter later."

Vito got into his car and moved ahead, finding a place to pull to the curb to allow the other vehicle to pass. Then, seconds later, he was right by her side again. She'd found a crumpled napkin, rather than opening her own medical kit, because the wound wasn't all that bad. But Vito came toward her as if she'd been seriously injured. "Let me see."

"It's fine, it's—"

"What happened to your face?" he asked, gazing at her in horror.

She felt the scratch on her cheek. It wasn't all that bad, really. "Nothing, just a rescue attempt gone bad last night."

He poured some antiseptic onto a cotton ball and said, "You went without me? You should've called—"

"Vito, I'm fine by myself," she said, wincing from the sting of the antiseptic as he swabbed her knee. He was a heavy hand, so she took it from him and applied it on her own. "Besides—"

"Yeah, but I could've helped you."

She fell silent. How fine was she by herself? She hadn't gotten anything but that scratch. Maybe she really did need his help. She took the bandage he offered and adhered it to the cut, then got to her feet.

"Can I give you a ride to the shelter?" he asked as she grabbed the paper cup from the gutter and tossed it in a garbage can with the rest of the waste.

"Oh, no, actually, I'm going—"

"You're not going to the shelter?" He smirked. "Wait, are you still looking into Mauro's murder?"

She sighed. She knew that devilish look in his eye. He wanted to help. And get himself in more trouble. And that was the last thing Sabina needed. "No," she lied. "I'm just—"

"Yeah, you are!" he said smugly. "I can tell. Anyone ever tell you, you're a horrible liar, Dr. Smart? Where are you going? Have you learned anything new?"

She rolled her eyes to the sky. The boy clearly wasn't giving up. Besides, maybe he could help her. "Okay. Yes. I learned that Dr. Mauro's wife had served him with divorce papers several times, but he refused to sign. Did you know that?"

Vito nodded. "Yeah. The whole town knew that. Loretta Mauro's kind of crazy. She lives like some Hollywood recluse up in that old mansion. Anytime you see her, she's wearing these dark, movie-star glasses. But really, I haven't seen her in *months*. The last time I saw her, she almost killed Dr. Mauro with her car. Before that, she was feeding his clothes to the fishes at the end of the pier. She's a real piece of work, that one."

"So do you think she could've, maybe—"

"Maybe. Anything's possible. I doubt she'll answer if you just go up and ring the doorbell." He motioned to his car. "But come on. I'll give you a ride."

She hesitated on the sidewalk. "No. You go back to the shelter. I'm sure Sabina will—"

"Trust me. You'll want a ride. The place is on the edge of a cliff. You won't want to climb there."

She smiled. "All right. Thanks."

She stepped into the passenger side door and let Nick get in behind her. As they took off, he said, "Thought you were coming back to the clinic last night. I waited for you."

Oh, that's . . . nice, she thought, a little uneasy. "Sorry! It was a little crazy. Did Sabina say she saw me at dinner? I ate, and then I had the run-in with all those cats, and then I had to check on an electrocuted ferret, and then I had a meeting with Mauro's lawyer . . . it was a *day*."

He chuckled.

"Not to mention that my clinic in Mussomeli's blowing up!" she said with a little titter, though it pained her to think of poor Concetta, and the residents of Mussomeli, having to deal with the outbreak without her. "Turns out, they're in crisis. There may be rabies going around."

"No kidding?"

"Yeah. And my assistant, who is in veterinary school, might have it. So I'm a little on edge."

He nodded, again taking a curve way too fast, making Audrey nearly wind up in his lap. He went to nudge her back but his hand lingered there a second too long. She bristled as he said, "Maybe you should forget that place and stay here. With us."

"Vito. It's not that easy. I have a responsibility to—"

"Yeah. But you're good for this place. And we need you, too. You fit in with all of us. You belong here," he said. "Don't you think?"

She hesitated. Yes, people needed her here. She hated to think what poor Milo's family would've done if she hadn't been there. Without Dr. Mauro, any animal experiencing an emergency would be in big trouble. "A lot of Lipari thinks I'm a murderer."

"I don't. I'd never think that. If they arrested you, I swear, I'd . . ." He banged a fist on the steering wheel. "Well, I don't know what I'd do. Protest at the courthouse. Whatever. There's no way you could've done it."

She smiled at him. If only he'd be able to convince Officer Lorenzo. "That's very sweet of you. But Mr. Gallo will find someone else to take care of Lipari's pet population when I'm gone. I told him when he offered that I couldn't stay. I'm sure he's looking."

Vito pulled to an abrupt stop at a stop sign that made them both lurch forward. Thank goodness for seatbelts. Then he looked over at her. "No one else wants to come to this armpit. Sure, it's nice to visit, but when it comes to living here? Most people can't take it. But you can. You're the first normal person who's come here since I moved here."

His eyes were full of a strange sort of desperation. "Vito, I—"

"You should at least think about it."

She was about to say, *There's really no point,* but the poor kid had such a hopeful look in his eyes. His life hadn't been easy before. That was for sure. And maybe he saw her as an ally, the reason his life had gotten better. She hated to be the one to disappoint him, after everything he'd done to help her.

"Fine. I will. But right now . . . where is Loretta Mauro's home?" She looked around. They were on a hillside above the village, surrounded by trees.

He let out a big sigh and threw the car into drive. "Right up here."

She saw what he meant about it being quite a climb. After a near forty-five-degree ascent, a large, modern white mansion came into view among the blooming trees. All boxy, straight lines and dramatic curves, it didn't fit in with the baroque architecture of the rest of the island. There were no shutters on the many massive windows, making it look a bit like a tiny skyscraper.

Vito grimaced at it as they pulled into a U-shaped drive with a fountain in the center and a landscape full of flowering trees and palms. "Behold the monstrosity."

"Wow. She lives here alone?"

"Alone with the souls of the misfortunate she collects," he said, adding a sinister laugh. Then he shrugged and started to take off his seatbelt. "I'm kidding."

Audrey held up a hand. "Stay here."

"What? No." He reached for the door. "What if she wants to add you to her collect—"

"For the last time, I'll be *fine,*" she told him. "Now, stay. You too, Nick."

Nick howled as she slipped out the door and closed it before he could jump out.

She went up to the door. The front stoop was covered with dried palm fronds and leaves, so thick that the welcome mat underneath was barely visible. Though there were open sidelights on either side of the door and so many windows in the house itself, it looked dark and foreboding inside. Even when she ran the doorbell, it let out a tinny, unwelcoming sound.

125

Audrey waited a moment and then looked back at Vito, who shrugged and mouthed, *I told you she wouldn't answer.* Nick had climbed onto the dashboard and was scratching at the windshield in vain, trying to escape and be part of the action.

She rang the doorbell again and shivered. The breeze up on this hill from the ocean was almost icy. Though the view beyond the palms was spectacular, the vistas stretching all the way toward Vulcano and Messina in the distance, it also gave her vertigo. Beyond the driveway and road was a precariously steep drop-off that made it feel sinister. As beautiful as it all was, she couldn't ever imagine living in such a place.

Just when she thought she was out of luck, there was a noise from inside. From the window, she could see a small form limping its way toward the door. It opened a few inches.

A woman with black hair streaked with white opened the door. She was impossibly thin, wearing large dark sunglasses and a crisp white pantsuit, giving the impression of an Audrey Hepburn in her later years. Her eyebrows were entirely drawn on in almost cartoonish black crayon, in a slanting way that looked rather angry. "*Si?*"

"Ms. Mauro?" she asked.

The woman whipped off her sunglasses to reveal eyes narrowed into wrinkled slits. "*Tu chi sei?*"

"*Scusi.*" She pointed to herself. "Dottore Smart. From America. I knew Dr. Mauro."

She rolled her eyes, uninterested. "I don't care. I have nothing to do with him anymore. And I have nothing to say to you, Dottore Smart."

"It's about his murder."

She stared at Audrey for a beat, and then opened the door wider. "Ah. You think I did it? If you did, you are Dottore Stupid, I should say." She snorted and waved an arm dramatically. "Ha! You think I care enough about him to throw away my life like that? You are wrong. You see, I care so little about him that I would never do such a thing. Look at me! I have the house. I have his money. I didn't need to kill him. I already had everything of his that was worth anything."

Audrey frowned. "I heard that he wasn't willing to grant you a divorce."

The woman's beady eyes zeroed in on Audrey, making her feel about two inches tall. "Yes. The fool. What . . . were you . . . and he . . .?"

Audrey shook her head, but before she could deny it verbally, the woman continued on.

"Did you want him to divorce me so that he could marry you? Is that it? Listen, little girl. I know very well of his affairs with other women. That pretty little tramp with the blonde hair that used to parade around his office in the short skirts and the tight tops. She thought she was something special, too. But no. And believe me, you were never going to get what you wanted from him. He was wholly devoted to me. Too devoted. I kept trying to untangle myself from his web and every time I did, he found a way to pull me back. We fought. All the time!" She laughed. "But that was our way. It was sport for us. Fun. I sent the divorce papers, and he didn't sign them. That was our game, too. And now that he's dead, I will miss all the fun."

"You're saying you got nothing from his death?"

"No. Not a thing that he didn't give me already. He might have made the money, but I managed it. I still do. He was silly. Never cared about that."

"He wasn't living here?"

"Oh, no. No, the two of us under the same roof? Not a good thing. And I'm—how do you say?—*allergic* to animals."

Audrey stared in surprise. "You married a veterinarian and you're allergic to animals?"

"Yes! I hate them! I can't get near them! Even when he'd come home from the office, he'd smell like animals. It'd start me . . ." She sniffled. Then she suddenly sneezed. She looked at Audrey through watery eyes. "*You* smell like an animal . . ."

The older woman's eyes wandered toward Vito's car and bulged.

"What is that?" She extended a claw-like, manicured finger toward Nick.

"He's a fo—"

Loretta Mauro sneezed again. "Oh no. No no no, I can't put up with this. I'm a virtual shut-in in my own home because I'm allergic to so many things. The air, the sunlight . . . but most of all, animals!" She went to close the door.

"One moment, please!" Audrey said, putting her hand on the door to stop her. "I just have one more question."

"Make it fast," she moaned, dabbing the sides of her eyes. "I can't take this much longer."

"Do you happen to know who might have wanted to kill him?"

"Me? No. Of course not, I have no idea."

Audrey wasn't so sure she believed that. She had to have known her husband was no angel. "But he had enemies, yes?"

127

"That's *two* questions," she muttered, and fluffed her dark hair, baring a massive diamond ring that covered most of her knuckle. "I don't know. I heard he had some trouble down at the clinic. A few patients that might not have been happy with his care. But I don't pay attention to his work. I've never even been in his office. Like I said, I'm allergic."

Audrey nodded. "All right. Thank—"

"But I did hear about a little spat he had with a new veterinarian, down near his office. Someone said it was pretty brutal," she said, a sly smile appearing on her face. "Was that you?"

Audrey swallowed. "It was, but—"

"Something tells me you have more of a motive than anyone else. Is that why you're here? Trying to find someone to pin it on so the police don't come after you?" She held up her hands. "Sorry to disappoint you, but I'm clean. You can't put anything on me. I never leave my house anymore. Ask anyone."

Just because no one saw you doesn't mean you weren't there, she thought, but before she could verbalize that, another thought hit her. Audrey's fight with Mauro had lasted barely two minutes, and yet all of Lipari knew it happened. It wasn't easy for anyone to keep secrets here. And Audrey had a hard time believing that a fragile, arthritic thing like Loretta Mauro could steal down this hillside without being noticed in order to kill her husband.

Or maybe she was just faking all this?

"Thanks for your—"

"I suppose you have a good motive, too, eh? You didn't like the competition from my ex-husband, hmm? He got in your way? And so you took him out?"

Audrey shook her head. "I'm just trying to find out what happened to—"

"You'd better run. They're onto you," she said, motioning behind her.

Audrey turned to see a police car pulling into the U-drive, right behind Vito's car.

Oh, no. They're after me again.

CHAPTER TWENTY FIVE

As Officer Lorenzo stepped out of the car, grimacing at Audrey, Loretta slammed the door closed.

"What are you doing here, Miss Smart?" Lorenzo said, shaking her head. She'd brought along one of the younger officers, the pretty blonde female.

"I was just—" Audrey looked around helplessly. Now she couldn't blame her appearance here on searching for strays. The allergic woman probably wouldn't be much help at all. She stammered, "Well, I—"

Vito jumped out of the car. "We're here because someone reported seeing some strays around here. That's all."

Officer Lorenzo gave him a look that was absolutely dripping with skepticism. "Right. Vito. Get back in the car."

"I'm serious," he said, hanging on the door.

"And so am I," she responded, going past him and nudging the door. He gave Audrey a sheepish look and slunk back behind the steering wheel.

Audrey said, "Why are you here?"

The blonde officer said, with a hint of pride, "We had a pretty hot lead come through."

"A hot lead? Really? Are you going to question Dr. Mauro's wife about his murder? Do you think—" She stopped as she noticed the papers in the officer's hand. She couldn't quite make it out, but did that say, *Mandato?* So was that an arrest warrant? "What is that?"

Officer Lorenzo pointed toward the car. "For once, Miss Smart, all signs are not pointing to you. So if I were you, I'd be happy. And *leave*, so we can carry on with our business."

Audrey backed away toward the car and grabbed ahold of the handle as Officer Lorenzo drummed her hands hard on the wooden door. She barked, "*Loretta Mauro! Apri la porta! Adesso!*"

Whatever the officers were there for, Audrey knew that this time, they meant business.

"Holy sh . . . cow," Vito murmured from inside the car as Audrey settled herself in, watching the scene intently. "Are they gonna arrest that old bag?"

"I don't know," Audrey whispered, as Nick made himself comfortable on her lap. "Maybe. They said something about a hot lead. And I think I saw an arrest warrant in the other officer's hand."

"Hot lead? Like what?"

"No clue. You'd think they already interviewed the ex before." *If they knew what they were doing, which . . . the jury is still out on that one.*

"Should we leave?" Vito asked, reaching for the key in the ignition.

She put a hand over his. "Just wait. A little longer . . ."

The door opened. Audrey could see Loretta, wearing her dark sunglasses again and frowning, clearly unimpressed and unafraid of her newest guests. Lorenzo spoke quietly. Loretta, on the other hand, launched into a rapid-fire Italian tirade that only seemed to get louder and louder the longer the officer stood there.

"What is she saying?" Audrey asked, since the only word she could make out was *Never.*

Vito rolled his window down some more, listening. "The police just served her with a search warrant. I think for Loretta's car."

"And what is Loretta saying?"

Vito winced. "You're a lady. I don't think you'd like me to repeat those words to you. But let's just say she isn't happy about it."

Loretta took the paper and scanned it. Then she threw up her hands and pushed open the door. Hobbling with the help of a cane, she followed the two officers out to the four-car garage across from them. As they walked, Loretta said, "What for? I don't lock it!" but there was a little back-and-forth, until Loretta finally handed the younger officer the keys and motioned to the first bay, still cursing loudly in Italian. The office lifted the door on the first garage bay to reveal a white, old-model Mercedes in pristine condition.

Vito whistled. "Look at that car. I haven't seen Loretta out driving that baby since I first got here. That was years ago."

Audrey squinted as the officers went deeper into the garage and opened the doors. A moment later, the trunk was popped, and Lorenzo leaned inside, moving things around. Meanwhile, Mrs. Mauro stood there, leaning on her cane and gesturing wildly with her free hand. From her tone of voice, Audrey gathered it was probably more words that "a lady shouldn't hear."

"Wow," Vito breathed.

"What?" Audrey asked him.

"Well, they've got to be pretty hard up if they think they're going to find something in there. That car probably hasn't been out of there in ages."

"You have to be wrong about that. How does she get her food and—"

"She has a girl bring it up to her. She doesn't leave the house. Hardly at all," he murmured, his hands wrapped around the steering wheel. "So where did this great lead come from? Because I'm telling you . . . if I was a police officer and someone told me to look in Loretta Mauro's car, I'd put that lead at the bottom of the pile. No way would I consider it a *hot* lead."

"Huh," Audrey said. "It doesn't seem credible, does it? Considering she doesn't exactly seem like—"

"But this is Lipari. I doubt they get many leads at all. They probably—" He stopped speaking as Officer Lorenzo lifted something out of the trunk. She reached into her pocket and pulled out an evidence bag, then stuffed the thing inside. "What's that?"

Audrey leaned closer. "It looks like a vial of medicine." She gasped. "I bet I know what kind."

Vito looked at her and they both spoke at the same time: "*Pentobarbital*." He blinked. "Whoa. Things are about to get *real*."

She nodded as Loretta stared at the thing in confusion and shouted, *"Cos'è quello. Non l'ho mai visto prima in vita mia!"* What is that? I've never seen that before in my life!

Vito said, "She's saying that she's never—"

"Thanks, but I got it," Audrey said as Lorenzo stepped away from the car and moved toward the doctor's wife, grabbing at her waist for her handcuffs.

To Audrey's disbelief, she motioned for the old woman to turn around. As she gently snapped on the cuffs, Loretta wailed in indignation. *Does this mean I'm off the hook?* Audrey wondered.

As she guided Loretta toward the police cruiser, Lorenzo gave Audrey the stink-eye. *Apparently not. Or maybe she's just upset because she told me to leave and I haven't yet. I haven't been very good at following her directions.*

"Um," Audrey said, nudging Vito. "We'd better go."

"Right." He started up the car, looking a little shell-shocked. "What just happened? Because unless I'm seeing things, they just arrested Loretta Mauro for murdering her husband."

Audrey blinked in disbelief. "I saw that, too," she said, still rattled as she watched the frail woman being placed in the back of the cruiser. "But come on. Let's go back to the shelter. I'm sure Sabina needs us."

"Yeah. But I really didn't see that one coming," Vito said, pulling away from the curb.

Neither did Audrey. But that was why she wasn't a cop. She was a vet. And she had a full day of catching more strays ahead of her.

*

Audrey yawned in the front passenger seat of Vito's car. After a busy day at the shelter, she was ready to call it a night.

"What are you thinking?" Vito asked her as he pulled up to her hotel. "About Loretta Mauro, huh?"

She nodded.

"Yeah. I agree."

She looked at him. "So you do think something about it is off? I mean, she was allergic. She never went to his office. She could barely walk. I mean, how could she—"

"Well, maybe she was just trying to throw us off the track, make everyone think that there was no way it could be her."

"I guess. It's just—I guess the police here really know what they're doing. For a minute there, I wasn't sure."

He snickered. "They don't really know what they're doing. Trust me. But I guess this time, they just got lucky."

"Yeah. Looks like it." She reached for the door and yawned again. "Thanks, Vito. For all your help."

He grinned. "No problem."

"I don't know what I'd do without you. Want to do some stray catching on the beach tomorrow, before we go to the shelter? Say, nine?"

"Yeah," he said, almost too readily. "Sounds great. It's a date."

Audrey laughed. "Okay, well . . . if you want to call it that."

His smile faded. "Hey, uh . . . you want me to come in for a little bit?"

She blinked. "What? No. I think I can find my way." She laughed. *What in the world is he thinking? Well, probably the same thing most eighteen-year-old boys are. It's not really a mystery.* "Have a good night."

She slammed the door and went into the lobby, still laughing to herself over Vito. Seriously, the island of Lipari was small, but it had to have some women more his age to choose from. Was he that hard-up that he was fawning over her, a woman old enough to be his mom? *Am I old enough to be his mom? Oh, god, I am! Perfect. That's just the type of proposition I'd expect. Meanwhile, men my age run in the other direction as fast as they can.*

She pulled out her phone when she pressed the button for the elevator and looked at her messages. One from Mason: *No sign of the infected dog. Concetta doing fine. How are you?*

Audrey typed in: *Doing fine. I think I might be coming home soon.*

Just as the elevator doors slid open, Councilman Gallo appeared in the lobby doors and waved at her. "Audrey!" he called.

She let the elevator go and went over to him. "Hello. How are you doing?"

"Fine, fine. I wanted to tell you how much I appreciated everything you've been doing in our humble home," he said with a warm smile. "I apologize for all the messiness where Dr. Mauro was concerned. I hope it didn't put you off too much."

"Not at all, Councilman."

"I was just speaking with the police and they have mentioned that they made an arrest in the case." His brow knitted. "Loretta Mauro. The doctor's estranged wife."

"I have heard, yes."

He shook his head, a troubled expression on his face. "Very odd, in my opinion. I knew Loretta, of course. For many years. In fact, we went to school together. I never thought she had it in her—well . . ." He seemed to break from his trance, and a smile appeared. "It's all over. Thank goodness. It was a very tense time for you as well, no doubt?"

"Yes, I'm sure that must be a relief for everyone."

"That means the police are not holding people here any longer, and you're free to go back to your home," he said reluctantly. "Have you thought any more about my offer?"

"Well, I've been really busy, so honestly, I haven't—"

"I'd love to get an answer soon. You know we'd take very good care of you."

She nodded. She had no doubt of that. She'd be a hero here. And she'd have the beach, and a chance to start over.

But she'd made a promise to the people of Mussomeli, and they needed her, too. Her father had always said to her that when she picked up a project, she needed to see it through. She was far from finished in the inland town, with her clinic and her little home.

"As lovely as it has been here, I do have to get back to Mussomeli. There is so much there I have to do."

"Yes." He pressed his lips together. "I was afraid you'd say that. And it's so unfortunate. Sabina says you've been a miracle worker. The pets really respond to you. I heard about that ferret you rescued, yes?"

"Rescued? Milo? Oh, no. That poor little baby just had mild burns from electrocution. I think he will be f—"

"Yes, but it's not just Milo. Everyone's talking! Our pet population is already showing signs of improvement due to your efforts. I couldn't be happier. You'll always be welcome here in our humble little village."

"Thank you. I'd love to come back again."

"So, you will be leaving soon?"

She shook her head. "Not right away. I'm going to do some stray catching tomorrow and finish up a few more things at the shelter. But I'll probably leave the day after, if that's all right."

"Oh yes! Any extra day we can have you in our presence is a good one!" he said, taking her by the shoulders and pulling her into a robust hug, then kissing her on each cheek. "It has been such a pleasure, Dottore Smart! I'll make sure we have a check for your efforts, ready and waiting for you when you leave!"

"Thank you for all your hospitality," she said as he turned and headed out the lobby doors.

She went back to the elevator and pressed the button, then glanced at her phone. She had a message from Mason: *Can't wait to see you, Boston.*

She groaned inwardly. There he was, saying those sweet things to her and ensuring that all she'd probably do when she went to bed was think of him. *Damn him.*

But when the elevators opened, she found herself dwelling on something else, something that Councilman Gallo had said: *I never thought she had it in her.*

That makes two of us, Audrey thought.

134

CHAPTER TWENTY SIX

"Good morning," Audrey said sleepily as she met Vito outside the following day at precisely nine a.m. He had everything ready to go—the crates, extra food to lure the cats, and of course, plenty of latex gloves. The kid was certain prepared for this. "Wow. Look at you."

He studied her. On the other hand, she couldn't stop yawning, and felt dead on her feet. She needed coffee, big-time.

"You don't look like you're ready to do some stray-hunting, Doctor," he said with a teasing lilt to his voice. "What happened? Bad night?"

"Something like that. But I'm fine. It was a great night. I just didn't sleep well, for some reason." She side-eyed him. "What about you?"

"I always sleep like a rock. Well, when I do go to sleep. I was up playing Call of Duty until three in the morning."

Oh. So that answered that question. She'd been wondering if he'd thought more about Loretta Mauro's arrest. Something about it—something Audrey couldn't put her finger on—seemed so strange. She thought he'd agreed with her last night. But now, it seemed as if he hadn't even given it a second thought. "Didn't you think yesterday was weird?"

"What? Mauro being arrested for killing her husband?"

"Yeah. You said she was a recluse. And she was so frail."

He shrugged. "Sure. But I also know she's a few sandwiches short of a picnic. Never underestimate the crazy and their infinite capability to surprise. I mean, look at Nonna. On the surface, she looks pretty normal. No one would think she spent last night putting on *Romeo and Juliet* with the shelter cats in lead roles."

Audrey's eyes widened. "She did?"

He nodded. "She makes little costumes for them and everything." He reached down and picked up some of the equipment. "So yeah, does Loretta Mauro look like a cold-blooded killer? No. Could she have murdered her husband? Yeah. Possibly. So just let the police sort it out."

"I guess you're right."

She picked up some of the food and a few crates and followed him down the street toward the beach, not wanting to talk any more about it. It was what had gotten her worked up last night. She'd been turning over Loretta Mauro's arrest in her head, letting it tumble about her mind like clothes in a dryer. The more she did, the more wrong it felt. Yes, maybe Loretta Mauro had been milking her disability, and maybe she wasn't as much of a recluse as she'd made herself out to be. But still . . . very little escaped this town's notice. If a woman as striking and interesting as Loretta Mauro had appeared downtown, near Dr. Mauro's office . . . people should have noticed.

But they hadn't. Which meant that either she'd been really good at escaping detection, or . . . she wasn't the killer.

Ugh. Why am I bothering thinking about it? Vito's right! I should just leave it in the hands of the police.

But were the police really acting on solid information? Where had that lead even come from? They weren't professional case-crackers. And that vial of pentobarbital, so conveniently placed in Loretta Mauro's unlocked car, in an unlocked garage?

She hated to admit it, but it had all the markings of a plant. How easy would it be for the real killer to put that vial in there, and sway the police Loretta's way.

"You don't think—" She was so busy thinking that she barely noticed that Vito was holding a breakfast pastry and coffee out to her. "Oh. Thanks." She took it. "You're—"

"A lifesaver. I know." He took a sip of his own coffee and said, "I don't think what?"

"I was just thinking about that vial."

He raised an eyebrow. "What about it?"

"I was thinking it was really convenient that the police found it there."

"Well. They had a lead."

"Right. But from where?"

They reached the corner. The sun was just rising over the rocky jetties on either side of the small beach, and the water itself was mirror-calm. The sky was a pretty shade of pink, and full of seagulls, their forlorn calls mixing with the comforting sound of the waves, swishing lightly on the shore. It was a beautiful day, quiet and calm, before the first ferry of the morning and the tourists arrived.

Audrey spotted Vittoria Vittelo canvassing the shore, her head down. Audrey waved, but the woman was too absorbed in whatever she was doing. She stopped, crouched, picked something up, and stuck it in her canvas bag.

"Speaking of crazy," Vito said under his breath, heading to the beach. "She and my Nonna are two peas in a pod. Come on. I think I saw a couple of strays heading under the pier."

"All right."

She followed him toward the pier, trudging through the dark sand. When they reached the shade of it, surely enough, she noticed a few sets of glinting cat eyes peering back at her.

"Okay," she instructed Vito, as Nick arrived on the scene, ready to help. She smiled. "Always right on time, aren't you, Nick? I'm going to ease in slowly. You two go over to each side of me so that you can intercept them in case they try to make a run for it. Got it?"

Vito clapped his hands. "Ready. Let's do this."

They got into position on the beach and slowly advanced forward, toward the pier. Audrey did so with a little more care, still feeling the sting on her cheek from her last attempt. When she got to the end of the boarded walkway, she ducked her head underneath and extended one of the cat treats she kept in her pocket.

Almost too easily, the young male cat came forward and took the bait. She scooped him up and gave a triumphant squeal of excitement. Vito grabbed one of the cardboard crates and assembled it so she could drop the cat inside, and put the lid atop. "Voila!" Audrey said.

Vito held up a hand for her to high-five. "Let's go get another."

The next one seemed encouraged by its brother's actions, because he was just as easy to catch, using almost the exact same method. But this time, when Audrey scooped him into her arms and turned, it wasn't Vito waiting for her with a crate.

It was Vittoria.

"Oh, hi," she said, noticing Vito down the beach, trying to assemble the crate.

"Capturing kitties, eh?" Vittoria said with a shake of the head.

Audrey sighed. "Yes. I know what you said about them liking their freedom. But we will free them, after we neuter them. They'll be very humanely treated."

"They didn't do anything. Just like Loretta. And they captured her, too."

Audrey stopped wrestling with the wriggling kitten. "What do you mean?"

"You know they have the wrong person. Don't you?"

Audrey shook her head, but even as she did, she couldn't deny it. It was true. All last night, something had not sat right with her. Whenever the police had caught the culprit, everything seemed to fall into place. But right now? Something did seem off. She'd said it from the beginning. "Then who did it, do you think?"

Vittoria shrugged. "But don't let that old lady stay in jail, when she do nothing wrong. That's criminal."

"How do you know?"

"I know Loretta. Know her all my life. She no like her husband, fought him all the time, but she's not a murderer. She don't hurt a fly. I tell the police that. They shoo me away."

At least someone was thinking the same way Audrey was, even if it was the town crazy lady. "Well, I'm sorry. I don't know what I can do, Vittoria. I'm not a police officer. I'm not supposed to get involved."

"Bah. The police know nothing. They arrest the wrong lady. They know she couldn't have done it and they don't care. They don't let me tell them nothing. They as pig-headed as Dr. Mauro was!"

She meandered away, muttering under her breath, as Vito approached with the new cardboard crate. Audrey set the cat inside as Vito watched the old lady leave. "Told you she was batty. What was she saying to you?"

"She was telling me that she didn't think Loretta Mauro murdered her husband," she murmured, watching the old lady lean down to pet another stray cat.

Vito fastened the lid on the top of the crate and looked up at her. "And let me guess. Based on what you were saying before . . . you don't think Loretta Mauro did it either?"

"Well . . . what do you think?"

He tilted his head. "I thought it was weird to begin with, to be honest. But they already arrested her. I'm sure they'll question her, and if they have reason to believe she didn't do it, they'll let her go. Right?"

"I don't know. Maybe not," she said. "They don't exactly seem like they handle this kind of thing all the time."

"They don't," Vito agreed. "But what can you do?"

Audrey gnawed on her lip, then backed away toward the street, as the idea came to her. Of course—she needed to know where that lead came from. And to do that, there was only one place she had to go. "I don't know. But hey. Do you think you can take care of getting these cats to the shelter?"

Vito frowned. "Yeah, but . . . Wait. What are you going to do?"

"I'm going to go to the police station and have a talk with Officer Lorenzo," she said, breaking into a run. Suddenly, though, she stopped and turned. "Uh, Vito? Could you tell me exactly where the police station is?"

CHAPTER TWENTY SEVEN

In a small village on the sea like that of Lipari, it wasn't difficult to find the police station. Audrey stumbled upon it right where Vito said it would be, on the other side of the main drag, past the harbor restaurant. As expected, it wasn't much of a station, just a crumbling, narrow stone house, with a sign outside that said *Polizia.* Audrey might have passed by it altogether if it weren't for the single police cruiser parked outside.

She stepped inside, thinking it would be bustling like any normal police station, but she was wrong. There was a single unoccupied desk in the room, and no human life in sight. "Hello?" she called, and her voice echoed through the empty room.

The brawny male officer stepped in from a back room, giving her a surly look. He was holding a mug of coffee and a pastry. "Oh, it's you," he said, taking a bite of it. "What do you want?"

"Good morning to you, too," she said with a smile. "I just wanted to—"

"Officer Lorenzo said you might be poking around in here. And if you did, I was to turn you away." He set his breakfast on the desk and sat down, then made a flicking motion toward the door. "So . . . go. The tourists are going to be arriving soon. They always bring trouble."

"Is Officer Lorenzo here?"

He let out a groan. "Did you not hear me?"

"I did. But I'd like to talk to her. I have an issue I'd like to raise."

"She doesn't want to talk to you. And besides, she's not here. She doesn't come on until the afternoon."

"Oh, is she—"

"Lipari has three police officers. We alternate shifts. I'm the one in charge now. And I'm telling you to get out, unless you want to wind up in handcuffs. Because that can be arranged."

She fought the urge to back away. "I'm sure it can. I know you arrested Loretta Mauro for the murder of her husband."

A smile spread over his face. "Yep. Excellent bit of police work, that was."

"Was it? You don't think she actually did it, do you?"

His brow knitted. "What do you mean? Of course she did. We found the smoking gun right there in her car. She's guilty."

"Right. What made you three decide to get that warrant to search her car again? Was it just dumb luck?"

He scoffed. "Of course not. It was a tip."

"A tip? From who?"

"It was an anonymous tip."

Audrey rolled her eyes. Just as she'd expected. "You took the call?"

He nodded.

"So you don't have any idea who gave you that tip?"

"No," he said, as if it were an absurd question. "Of course not."

"Did you ask?"

He spread his palms on his desk and stood up. "No. She hung up before I could. But listen, *Signorina* . . ."

"So it was a *she*? A woman?"

He pressed his lips together, as if just realizing he'd said too much. "You need to go—"

"I'm just confused as to why you wouldn't question where this anonymous tip came in from. The fact is that Loretta Mauro's car was unlocked, in an unlocked garage. That means that anyone could have planted the vial there. You ever think of that? Or of the fact that her Mercedes rarely leaves the garage, and she hasn't been spotted in town in months? She has someone to do her shopping for her, and—"

"Get out!" the officer said, red-faced, banging his fists so hard on the desk that his coffee sloshed all over his papers. "Loretta Mauro has been arrested for this crime, and that's all I'm going to say!"

He'd already said enough. Now Audrey was surer than ever as she left the police station.

Loretta Mauro had been framed. By a woman, the woman who'd made the phone call.

But who?

As Audrey wandered down the sidewalk toward the pier, she tried to think of who it could possibly be. Vittoria? No, it was likely she didn't even have a phone. And Vittoria seemed to like Loretta, and think that she was innocent. Why would she say such a thing if she'd framed her? Besides, she'd been at a protest.

Sabina? That was a possibility. As batty as the old woman was, she might have done such a thing. And she knew how to use pentobarbital, too. But she'd been with Vito while the murder was taking place, so unless he was lying—and Vito didn't strike her as the type to lie about something like that—she probably couldn't have done it either.

A bicycle horn honked, stirring Audrey from her thoughts. She found herself meandering in the street by the pier, just as a ferry was arriving. The ship was full of tourists, all jockeying to be the first to leave the boat and enjoy their day in Lipari. Soon, the relatively bare streets, shops, and restaurants would be crowded with people.

She walked a little farther up the street, toward the shelter, still lost in her thoughts. Who else had access to pentobarbital, knew how to use it, and had the motive and opportunity to commit the murder?

A group of young tourists who looked like college students suddenly tore past Audrey on both sides, nearly knocking her over. They were conversing loudly in another language she couldn't quite place. As they did, one of them tossed a balled up receipt on the ground.

"Really?" Audrey shouted after them, calling to mind something her father used to say to her and Brina whenever they came in and dropped their book bags in the front foyer at the end of a day. *If I have to stop and pick that up, I'm going to knock you into the beginning of next week.* "You going to pick that up?"

They ignored her and continued on as the piece of refuse rolled on the breeze, up the street.

Audrey shook her head. "Slobs," she muttered, looking around for Vittoria. If she were here, she'd give those kids a stern talking to. *It's people like them who give tourists a bad name,* she thought, rushing after the paper as it skittered across the sidewalk, coming to rest beside a building.

Just as she reached it, the wind picked up and blew it down the street.

"Oh, fantastic," she mumbled, straightening and running after it again. She'd nearly gotten a hold of it when it when flying once again, this time into a gutter that was full of stagnant brown water. There, it stayed, sinking into the muck. "Gross."

Audrey reached in and plucked it up with her thumb and forefinger. Now that she was close to it, she realized it was an old ferry receipt. But it was so heavy and brown with dirty water that much of it was illegible. Turning, she looked for the nearest public trash can, when a strange sense of déjà vu gripped her.

The files. Mauro's files. They'd fallen into a puddle, ruining them. Not that it mattered much. There was nothing in there that was very helpful.

Except . . .

Suddenly, the name came to her. *Flora . . .* something. The vet tech or receptionist who'd worked for Dr. Mauro. Her name had been all over the files. She'd prepared them for him. Audrey had meant to ask Vito or Sabina about her, but with all the chaos, it'd slipped her mind.

Quickly, she reached into her purse and pulled out the file.

Flora Abruzzo.

Suddenly, something that Loretta Mauro had said came to Audrey's mind, clear as day: *I know very well of his affairs with other women. That pretty little tramp with the blonde hair that used to parade around his office in the short skirts and the tight tops. She thought she was something special, too.*

Of course. The vet tech. Was Dr. Mauro having an affair with the vet tech? If she had been jilted in some way, which caused her to leave her job . . .

This was a *definite* lead.

Hands shaking with her excitement, she picked up her phone and called the shelter. A male voice answered, nearly drowned out by the breeze and the sound of tourists walking about. *"Lipari rifugio per animali. Vito."*

"Vito?"

"Audrey? Is that you? Where are you? Sounds like you're in a wind tunnel. I thought you were coming back to the—"

She squeezed her ear closed to block out the voices of the tourists who were scattering across the main street, peering in the shop windows and heading off to breakfast at the cafés. "No. I'm still by the pier."

"Did you go to the police? Did you find something?"

"Yes. Well, maybe. I don't know. But listen to me. I need your help. I have a question for you," she said hurriedly, looking around. The streets were now crowded with the newcomers, moving along the sidewalks, viewing the different shop windows, but she was the only one standing still. She moved aside so they wouldn't mow her down. "Do you know a Flora Abruzzo?"

"Flora . . ." He paused. "Abruzzo? Yeah. Sure. She worked for . . .Wait—"

"Do you know where she lives?"

143

"Yeah. Uh—she lives in the apartments across from Mauro's clinic. The ones with the blue shutters. I don't know where exactly. But Audrey—"

"And she worked as a vet tech for Dr. Mauro?"

"A while ago, yeah. Maybe like six months ago. I don't think she's been with him for a while."

"Do you know what happened?"

"No. I guess she moved on. But—"

"I've got to go. I'll talk more later," she said quickly, ending the call.

This was it. Of course. A woman, with a knowledge of how to use pentobarbital and the ability to get it. But did she have the motive—was she having an affair with the doctor? And had she had the opportunity?

Audrey couldn't wait another second. She had to find out.

CHAPTER TWENTY EIGHT

Audrey hurried up the street, Nick scampering at her heels, until she found Dr. Mauro's office. Sure enough, consistent with Vito's directions, there was a small, attractive apartment complex across the way, a white stucco building with blue shutters and an arched corridor in the center behind a gate, where there were blue doors on either side.

"Stay here, Nick," she whispered to her fox as she tried the latch on the gate. It lifted.

Audrey pushed the gate open and went inside. The first door was surrounded by terra cotta pots full of succulents and flowers. There was a doorbell, and underneath it, the name, written in black print: *Abruzzo*.

First time's a charm? That's rare for me, Audrey thought with a smile as she knocked on the door. Every win of hers usually came with enormous effort. *Maybe this is a sign of good things to come.*

It was the middle of the day, so she didn't expect an answer. So she was surprised when the door opened to reveal a pretty girl with strawberry blonde hair and light eyes. Probably in her mid-twenties, she was wearing a bra top and bike shorts, her skin flushed as if she'd just gotten in from a run.

"Si?" she said, tilting back a container of water and gulping it.

"Miss Abruzzo?" she asked.

The woman nodded. *"Ti conosco?"* Do I know you?

"No, you don't know me. I'm sorry if I bothered you, but . . ." Audrey hesitated. *Did you murder Dr. Mauro* sounded a little abrupt. She'd have to find a different tack. Unfortunately, as she stood there, her mind went blank.

She wiped the sweat from her forehead. "It's all right. Are you American?"

Suddenly, an idea popped into Audrey's head. "Yes! I am an American, new to the island. I'm actually a veterinarian. Dr. Mauro's replacement. I'm looking for a good vet tech who speaks Italian and can help me with my new practice. I understand you worked for him before?"

"I did," she said carefully. "But I quit four months ago."

"Did you? The person I spoke to didn't know if you quit or were fired."

She shook her head, and her tone was slightly abrupt, bordering on offended. "No. I quit. I'm in between jobs now. You're looking for another tech?"

Audrey nodded. "Oh, then this might work out! You do speak Italian? I need someone who does, since—"

"Of course." She looked up and down the hallway. "But right now, I'm not ready for an—"

"Oh, no, it's fine. I thought we could have a formal interview later in the week, if you're available," Audrey said, looking past her into the apartment, unsure of what she was hoping to find. A bottle of pentobarbital there among her house plants? No, smoking guns like that only came that easily when the evidence was planted. "Does that work for you?"

"I guess, but—"

"Why did you quit your last job with Dr. Mauro, may I ask?"

She sighed. "Well, I don't want to speak ill of the dead, but Dr. Mauro had some problems. But I worked for him for six years. And then things changed. I didn't like it. So I told him I was quitting."

Audrey nodded. "Ah. He must've been upset to lose you. What do you mean, things changed?"

"The vet was going downhill. People were upset. The work environment was a hostile one. It wasn't fun to go to work anymore. So I had enough. And I left him."

Left him. Not *left the job.* Suddenly, something occurred to Audrey. She said, "You two were close before that?"

"Well, as close as an employee and an employer could be after six years together," she said. "He was a very competent man. I thought he was very good at what he did."

"You must have been upset when you heard he died."

She nodded. "It was terrible. A shock."

"And with that pentobarbital? That must've really shaken you, huh?"

The woman visibly shuddered, and her eyes narrowed. She grabbed the door and started to close it. "Yes. . . but look. I'm not really sure I want to take another job right now. So maybe we should—"

"I understand," Audrey said, trying to think quickly. "But maybe you could help me. I'm trying to look into licensing requirements in the area, and I'm having trouble, because it appears that Dr. Mauro's license is expired."

She nodded. "Yes. It was expired before I left there. He was a smart man but never very good at keeping up with the paperwork. I must've reminded him a thousand times to sign it. But he didn't." She rolled her eyes. "We could've gotten into a lot of trouble. But he didn't care. He was putting not only himself but *me* at risk. I told him that, but he didn't care. So we fought, and finally he just told me if I didn't like it, I should find another vet to work for. Stupid. There were no other vets on the island!"

Audrey blinked. "Wait. So you *were* fired?"

"No. Well . . . it was just a mutual separation, ah, agreement to part ways. But yes, I was a little bitter about the way we left things, if you must know. I was very good at what I did, and didn't deserve that kind of treatment."

Mutual separation? Now that sounded even more like a romantic relationship than a business one. "If you were fired, or felt you were wrongly terminated, you could've reported him to the authorities. An expired license would've been enough to close his operations down."

She shrugged. "Yes. But I didn't. I decided to let bygones be bygones. And—" She stopped and her brow wrinkled. "Who are you again? A vet? Why are you asking all these—"

"You were in a relationship with him, weren't you?" Audrey asked.

The girl's eyes went wide. "What? No!" She sighed. "All right, maybe we had a little something going on, but—"

"But he wouldn't leave his wife, right? And you were jealous? So you gave him an ultimatum, and he decided he wanted her. He fired you."

The woman's face had been getting significantly redder, even more flushed than it was from the exertion of whatever exercise she'd been doing. "Look I don't know what you're talking about—"

"That's why you never reported the expired license. Because it went beyond that. It wasn't enough to see him shamed for his business collapsing. You want him dead. And you wanted to frame his wife for it," Audrey said, her voice steadily rising. "Admit it."

"Fine! I did it!" she shouted. "I killed him and I'm not sorry. Not the least bit!"

CHAPTER TWENTY NINE

Audrey stared at Flora Abruzzo in shock, not sure she'd heard the woman right. Had she just admitted to murder? So easily? Just like that? "You . . . did it?"

The woman shrugged nonchalantly. "So what? You have absolutely no way of proving it. If you ask me to tell the police, I'll deny it."

Audrey looked up and down the hallway. Sure enough, there was no one there. No witnesses to corroborate her confession. It was just her word against Flora's. "But . . . how . . .?"

She sighed and once again looked up and down the hallway. "Why don't you come inside? If you must know, I'll tell you everything."

That's probably not a wise idea, Audrey thought, but the woman walked back inside, leaving her there, as if she didn't care what Audrey did.

Audrey hesitated for a moment. She could go and get the police, but then what? Flora would simply stonewall her and deny everything. But if she went in, maybe she could convince Flora to confess. She was just a young girl, after all, in her mid-twenties. She'd likely been wracked with guilt over the whole thing, and was happy to have everything out in the open.

Taking a deep breath, Audrey followed her into the apartment. Despite the rustic look of the outdoors, the apartment was modern, with dark wood laminate floors, white walls, and minimalist furniture. It was clear the girl had money.

Flora motioned her to an uncomfortable-looking, straight-backed sofa with chrome accents. Audrey lowered herself onto the cushion; it was just as stiff as it looked.

"Can I get you something to drink?" Flora asked. "Espresso?"

Audrey shook her head. *This is bizarre. I accuse her of murder, and she offers me an espresso. But this is good. If I play the "friend" angle, maybe I can convince her to confess.*

The girl sat down on a wicker chair across a thick, furry white area rug from Audrey. "All right. It's like this. How do these things ever start? I worked for Dr. Mauro right after getting my training in Rome. He was everything to me. A family friend, and a mentor. I was young and naïve and really looked up to him. A few years after we started working together, I realized he was spending time in the apartment over his clinic. I found out that he and his wife were having a hard time. Fighting a lot. She was accusing him of cheating on her, with me, I guess. She was acting all crazy toward him, making his life a living hell.

"So, we would talk about it. Yes, he's twenty-five years my senior, but when we spoke, we realized we had so much in common. I've always been an old soul, and he was so sad when he talked about Loretta. She didn't love him. He tried and tried to get her to show him love, but she was so cold," Flora said, her voice hollow. "Just a real bitch. I felt sorry for him. And eventually, it became physical. We fell in love. He told me that he loved me, that he wanted to leave Loretta and marry me. She found out about it and went even crazier, tossing him out of the house. But even though he ran to me, and we were in love, he told me he still loved Loretta and couldn't leave her. Stupid man. His loyalty was his downfall. He would do anything for her."

The girl's hands shook as she spoke. Audrey's breath shivered as she let it out. For the first time, she wished she'd brought Nick inside with her. He'd gotten her out of some scrapes before. "So then what happened?" she asked carefully, her eyes darting to the exit.

"I gave him an ultimatum. I told him it was either her or me. And he chose her. Probably because the bitch had a handle on his purse strings. He made the money, but she controlled it. She controlled everything. He fired me and told me that he would give me money to leave town, to go away from here. He just could not bring himself to leave his heartless *bitch* of a wife," she snarled, her face reddening.

Audrey swallowed. This wasn't good. The woman was getting riled. She needed to calm her down. *Agree with her.* "She sounds terrible. I'm so sorry that you were put in such an awful position."

Flora nodded. "Right? At first, I thought that I could get rid of her. Just sneak into her place and end her. Then he and I could be together. But the more I thought about it, the more I realized that both of them had taken everything away from me. I was going places. I was going to go for my doctorate, too, to become a veterinarian. But then he came along, and all I could think about was him. For what? It was worthless. A waste of my time. My life. The two of them took everything from me. They ruined me. So why shouldn't they both pay?"

"And then?"

She shrugged. "I called and told him I wanted to talk to him. I went to his office and met him there after hours. And I had the needle waiting. He didn't even know what hit him. If you use enough of it, that pentobarbital will kill before the patient realizes what is happening. And he paid. Just like I told him he would."

Audrey stared at her. Flora Abruzzo clasped her hands in front of her, shaking even more. The woman was clearly desperate. In a way, Audrey understood that. She'd had plenty of men pretend to understand, only to use her in the end and then easily discard her. The pain was almost unbearable, so that's probably why her heart squeezed for the poor girl.

"My God," Audrey whispered, not sure what to say. So she repeated herself: "I'm so sorry he hurt you."

Flora looked at her with tears in her eyes, blinking them away. "Yeah. Me, too."

"But murder is never the answer."

Flora shrugged. "It was for me. Now, the doctor is in hell where he belongs, and that bitch will hang for it."

Audrey stiffened. Those were clearly not the words of someone who regretted her actions. Audrey thought of Mason, and the way he'd looked at her at the door of his house, when she realized his betrayal.

It had hurt. So bad, she could barely breathe.

But never once had she considered such a drastic answer, creeping into Mason's house and committing cold-blooded murder. "You need to confess what you told me to police. That's the only way you can find peace."

A smile broke out on her face. "What makes you think I'm not at peace right now?"

In the girl's cold expression, Audrey saw something she'd never noticed before. Resolve. It chilled Audrey to the bone. "But . . .You can't be serious. You can't let Loretta Mauro take the blame for something you did!"

The woman stared at her. "Why not?"

"Because it's wrong. You must know that. How do you think you'd be able to sleep at night?"

She snorted and stood up, taking her bottle of water behind Audrey to the kitchen. Audrey heart the faucet go on, like she was rinsing out the bottle. "Like a baby?"

"But you wouldn't get away with it," Audrey said, trying to talk sense into her.

150

"You want to bet? I don't see anyone around here who's going to stop me."

Okay, so much for the "Be a friend" plan to get her to go running to the police. Think, Audrey. Before she could, she whirled on the sofa and her heart stopped.

Flora was standing there behind her, holding a full syringe. "What's that?"

Flora smiled at it. "You said you're a vet. I think you can figure it out."

"Yes . . . but what do you have it for?" she asked, her words trembling as they left her.

"What do you think? Don't be stupid, Doctor. I have enough pentobarbital to go around. Dr. Mauro trusted me implicitly. He let me take whatever I wanted from his medicine cabinet. In fact, he let me have the key to it. That's how I got the stuff that killed him. He was such a chump, he never knew it was missing."

Audrey slipped off the sofa and backed to the wall. "What are you going to do with that?"

Now, Flora laughed and put a finger on the plunger. "You really thought I was just going to tell you all that and let you go? I can't let you leave now."

"But . . . I won't tell anyone," Audrey begged, staring at the syringe as the woman took a step closer.

"Right. One thing that my time with Dr. Mauro has shown me?" She grinned wider, baring perfectly straight, white teeth. "Don't trust doctors."

Without warning, the woman lunged forward, moving around the sofa, toward Audrey. Audrey pushed away from the wall and ran, frantic, for the door. She hit it and scrabbled at the doorknob, managing to open it just an inch before Flora slammed against her back, shoving the door closed again.

Audrey spun halfway and grabbed the woman's wrist in her hand, just as she attempted to sink the needle in. The two scuffled there, holding each other still. Flora grunted, her eyes wild with hate as she held the syringe between them, trying to shove it into Audrey's neck. The syringe shook between them as Audrey held it off, but little by little, no matter how hard she tried to keep it away, it seemed to move closer to her neck.

She let out a scream as she felt the needle, first scraping, then starting to pierce the skin of her throat. *Oh, no. I'm dead. This is not going to end well,* she thought frantically as she sensed Flora moving her thumb to press the plunger at the end of the syringe. She felt the pressure digging into her body, anticipating the warm, poisonous liquid that would invade her veins and stop her heart.

Suddenly, a voice shouted, *"Polizia!"*

The voice had come from the outside hallway. Muffled, somewhat far away, but distinct nonetheless.

Flora's eyes, once full of determination, now widened with fear. The small blip in her concentration gave Audrey the distraction she needed to shove the needle away. With all her strength, she pushed with her forearms, letting out an animal grunt. Flora stumbled back, dropping the needle to the ground, and Audrey reached for the door just as it exploded open.

There was Officer Lorenzo, gun drawn, looking every bit like the police officer she'd been trained to be. Ready, and right on time.

At that moment, the room began to spin. Audrey felt faint, and the edges of her vision began to blur as the officer rushed in. Breathing hard, doubled over, Audrey pointed at Flora Abruzzo and the syringe while clutching at her heart with the other hand. She spat out, "Loretta Mauro's innocent. She's the one! Flora Abruzzo killed Dr. Mauro!"

CHAPTER THIRTY

Still breathing hard, Audrey tried to straighten, but the pain in her chest was a lightning rod. Had she gotten the medication inside her? Her heart was going a mile a minute. Clutching at it, she watched as Officer Lorenzo advanced on Flora Abruzzo. She pulled out her handcuffs and snapped one on Flora, then spun her around as expertly as any police officer Audrey had ever seen. Maybe she was more knowledgeable than Audrey had given her credit for.

Meanwhile, Flora unleashed a torrent of Italian curses on them, spittle flying from her mouth. Audrey sucked in a breath, and another, until she felt better. Maybe it had just been a panic attack. If she'd been injected, she'd definitely be feeling *worse*.

"How did you know?" Audrey asked Officer Lorenzo, leaning over to pick up the needle of pentobarbital.

"Don't!" Lorenzo warned, holstering her gun as the other male officer appeared.

Audrey let it go.

"Pick the syringe up," Lorenzo instructed the officer. Then she said to Audrey, "When you left the station, he radioed me and told me what you were up to. I was on the tourist beat, so I decided to take some time to follow you and see what you were up to. Good thing I did, yes?"

Audrey tilted her head to the sky and said a little prayer of thanks that she was still okay. Her voice was barely a whisper. "Oh, yes. A very good thing."

Lorenzo handed Flora over to the officer, who led her outside, her head down. She shook her head. "Flora Abruzzo. Of course, Dr. Mauro's old vet tech." She looked at Audrey. "Are you going to tell me what happened?"

"Yes. I realized that she had to have been the killer, and the vial you found in the car was just a plant. Flora Abruzzo was in a relationship with Dr. Mauro. She wanted him to leave his wife, but he refused, and a few months ago, he fired her. So, out of jealousy, she decided to murder him and pin it on the wife."

"No kidding," the officer said with a shrug. "I'd all but forgotten about Ms. Abruzzo. In fact, I didn't even know she still lived here. I thought when she was fired, she left Lipari altogether."

Audrey smiled and sat down on the couch. As she did, Nick rushed in and jumped on her lap. As usual, he'd wanted to be her savior, but she'd left him outside. She stroked his fur. "I think maybe that's what she wanted you to think. She kept a low profile. I get the feeling she's been planning this ever since she was fired."

Officer Lorenzo nodded. "Wow. Well, thanks for ironing that out. To tell you the truth, I was never quite sure about Mrs. Mauro being the killer. It seemed wrong."

"Same to me. That's why I couldn't stay away. I'm sorry if I stepped on your toes. But it just goes to show you, a woman's intuition is a valuable thing," Audrey said.

Officer Lorenzo smiled and shook her hand. "You're leaving soon?"

Audrey nodded. She knew exactly what the officer was saying. *Thanks for your help with this case. Please be gone for the next one.*

And she certainly planned to be. At that moment, she couldn't wait to get back to Mussomeli.

*

The following morning, Audrey turned in her hotel key at the front desk. As Councilman Gallo had promised, he'd left her a check and a little note. She gawked at the amount—it was far more than she'd expected for a tiny village—and smiled at the note from the councilman:

Dearest Audrey,

Again, words cannot express how happy we are with the work you have done here. You are welcome here any time, for a day, a week, or forever! Though I was able to find a new veterinarian that will be starting here in the next few months, perhaps you wouldn't mind coming back to help out? It is your planning and expertise that we will ask this doctor to follow, as we think it has done wonders for our island. You are truly a miracle worker! Thank you again, and be safe in your travels!

Best wishes,
Councilman Gallo

Audrey folded the note carefully and pocketed it, thinking about everything she'd use the money for. She could expand the clinic, or maybe even open another location! Hire an animal control officer to help catch the strays! Maybe hire a contractor to finish the repairs on the house! The possibilities were endless, and she couldn't wait. She hoisted her travel bag on her shoulder, picked up her pet carrier, and stepped outside, ready to walk to the pier and board the ferry.

"Nick!" she called at the door, and like clockwork, he appeared. She set the carrier down, opening the front, and he backed away. She motioned forcefully inside. "Come on. It's time to go home."

He eyed her warily.

She reached into her pocket and pulled out a few apple slices she'd gotten from the hotel café. The second she laid them at the bottom of the cage, he eagerly jumped in.

"Good boy," she said, sealing it up.

When she stepped to the curb, though, she found Vito waiting for her. He waved.

She went to the window and looked in. "Hi, there. Come to wish me goodbye?"

He nodded. "Hop in, I'll drive you to the pier."

She put her things in the back hatch, then opened the door and slid inside. As she settled her purse on her lap, she noticed the bouquet of flowers on the dashboard. "Oh. Is that for me?"

He nodded and pulled away from the curb. It was kind of silly, the ride, considering the hotel was less than a block from the ferry, but at least with Vito, she'd have someone seeing her off at the pier. "You like them?"

She took them and smelled their sweet aroma. "Oh you two didn't have to do this. I was more than happy to help with getting the shelter under control. And I'm really happy that you don't have to deal with all those cats-run-amok—"

"No," he said seriously, his brow wrinkled. "Audrey. They're not from Sabina. They're from me. Just me."

She blinked. "Oh," she said, confused. But the way he was looking at her made all the pieces suddenly fall into place. "*Oh . . . but Vito . . .*"

"I know. I should've said something before. But I really don't want you to leave. So maybe you can think about coming back, and—"

"Actually, I might."

His voice went up an octave, full of hope. "Yeah?"

"Well, of course. There's good news. You probably haven't heard. Councilman Gallo said there's a new vet coming. So I might come and help train whoever it is, in the future. We'll have to—"

"No, that's not what I mean," he said, shaking his head. "I meant that I hoped you'd come back to see me."

She gritted her teeth and set the flowers on her lap. "Oh, well, sure. Of course I wouldn't come back without stopping to see you and Sab—"

"No, you don't get it. I—"

"I do. I really enjoyed being with you over the past few days. You're like my fam—"

"I kind of like you," he blurted, making Audrey's eyes widen. As much as she'd been expecting it, she'd hoped he wouldn't go there.

But he'd gone there.

Shoot.

She'd known that was where he was heading, and she'd hoped to stop him from putting it all out on the table. But he was so earnest and young and passionate, of course he would. He was like a volcano that couldn't keep its top on. Now, her hand on his shoulder felt entirely inappropriate.

She quickly removed it as he continued on, "And *not* like family. I know. I'm a little younger than you. But—"

"Vito. You're a *lot* younger than me," she said, in her most mature voice. "I know I might not look it, but I'm almost thirty-five."

His eyes went wide; clearly, that wasn't something he'd expected, but they only stayed that way for a blink. Then he said, "I don't care. I think that you're incredible, Audrey. Like, the most incredible person I've ever met. And I . . . I . . . don't want you to leave."

Audrey smiled sadly. He was so sweet. And maybe if he were ten years older . . . "Vito. I'm really flattered. And I think you're an incredible k . . . uh, person, too. But it's not just the age difference. It's the distance, and everything . . . and you have your whole life ahead of you. There are so many experiences waiting out there for you. And with everything you've done, I can tell . . . you're not that kid people thought you were. That troublemaker? That's not who you are. You're going to do amazing things. If you want to study to be a vet, be a vet. You're going to blow people away. I promise you."

He nodded. "All right, all right." He laughed a little. "I figured you'd say something like that. But I had to take my shot."

Audrey laughed. "Okay . . ."

"Anyway, I'm applying to colleges in the States for next semester. Thinking about going back for biology with a concentration in animal sciences. You agree?"

She nodded. "Sure. I did that at BC."

"Can I hit you up for a recommendation?"

"Absolutely!" she said enthusiastically. She was *especially* enthusiastic to have the conversation swerve away from him wanting to date her. "Just give me a call! Anytime. And if you're ever in Sicily . . . look me up, all right?"

"Yeah. I will."

She held her hand out and he shook it. Then she scrambled out of the front seat of his car and got her things from the back, carefully balancing her belongings in her arms. She waved to him from the curb, then headed down the pier toward the gangplank to the waiting ferry.

She climbed up onto the top level of the ferry so that she could watch Lipari disappear from view. She placed her bags at her feet and went to the railing, still inhaling the scent of the flowers. As she did, her phone buzzed. It was a message from Concetta: *A hunter found the dog and brought him in! I just did a checkup on him and he's fine! No rabies!*

Audrey stared at the message. That was a relief. Now, she wouldn't have to worry about that when she got home. She typed in: *Amazing news! And I'm so glad you're going to be okay.*

Concetta responded a minute later: *Yes, going to open the clinic right now! When are you coming back?*

Audrey typed in: *On the ferry right now! Should get in tonight.*

She smiled when she saw the response: *Thank goodness! Mussomeli needs you!*

She sniffed the flowers again. The ferry blew its horn, sounding a low, mournful wail over the harbor as it began to pull away from the dock. Standing there in the sun, overlooking the rocky shore, Audrey saw Vito at the edge of the road, waving at her. She waved back. Down on the beach, still empty of tourists, Vittoria walked, canvassing the sand for treasures. The seagulls arced overhead in the pale blue sky, and the sun broke free of the rocky jetty, promising another beautiful day for the island.

She would miss it all. But there was someplace else that she missed more. And now it was time to return to it, the place where she belonged.

CHAPTER THIRTY ONE

The bus pulled into the main *piazza* in Mussomeli at shortly after nine in the evening. Audrey had been dozing, her head lolling against a window and feeling every bump, so when the brakes squealed and the bus came to a stop, she jolted upright and looked around. Through the dirty window, she could just make out the old fountain, and beyond that, several storefronts down *via Barcellona,* the sign that said *Veterinaria—Dott. Audrey Smart.*

Grabbing her things, she climbed off the bus. When she stepped off, she opened her carrier and let Nick out. He'd been so cooped up for the past few hours, and was so excited to be free, he practically ran to her little clinic. She ran, too, just as thrilled to be back.

Skidding to a stop in front of the place, she grabbed her keys, marveling at how the place still looked the same. *You're so silly, Audrey. Of course it still looks the same. You've been gone a few days. Not a year!*

But really, as shabby and low-frills as the place was, she couldn't imagine it looking better. She twisted the key in the lock and threw open the door, then looked around.

Just the same. Concetta and Mason had done a good job keeping everything in order.

The sound of animals barking and yipping greeted her ears. She meandered into the back room and turned on the lights. All the animals grew even more excited at the sight of her. There were a couple new ones, and some old friends. She went around, giving all of them pets, and checked on the bunnies. They were huge, now, almost ready to be put up for adoption. Yes, Concetta had done an amazing job.

But it hadn't been all her.

No, Mason had been there, too, for her.

As she thought of him, she noticed one of his blue sweatshirts, draped over a chair in the back office. She lifted it up, and on instinct, brought it to her nose and sniffed. It smelled like him, like that heady woodsy aftershave he always wore.

158

Yes, maybe they weren't ever destined to be lovers. Maybe he loved that other woman. But he'd come through for her. He was a true friend. He'd said he missed her, and she felt the same.

So why shouldn't she go over there, deliver his sweatshirt, and tell him she was back?

She checked the time on her phone. It was just after nine-thirty. He usually stayed up late. He'd be up. If his girlfriend was there, fine. She'd do the grown-up thing and ask to be introduced. That would be great.

Closing up the clinic, she headed toward the house. But instead of going straight to *Piazza Tre,* her home, she veered north, toward *via Milano.* Nick, walking two steps ahead of her, stopped and gave her a questioning look.

"Just one second," she told him, hoisting her bag higher up on her shoulder. "I have something to do first."

And this time, I hope I don't need to go home and console myself with a bowl of maccu di fave.

She stood outside his home, which was once again awash in light, fighting off those tendrils of déjà vu that threatened to sap away her courage. Taking a deep breath, she leaned forward and rapped on the door.

It opened at once, and this time, thank goodness, it was Mason who answered. "Hey!" he said again, once again, his voice full of surprised delight.

"Hey," she said, looking cautiously behind him. She couldn't see anyone else in there, but that didn't mean he was alone. "Am I interrupting anything?"

He shook his head. "No. Not at all." One of his eyes fell on Nick. "Oh, hey, Rat. I'm just—when did you guys get back?"

"Just now."

"Yeah?" That seemed to please him. He pointed behind him. "You want to come in?"

"Oh, no. It's fine. If you're *entertaining*—"

"I'm not, I'm alone," he said, and then let out a breath. Just as he did, Polpetto lumbered forward, clearly not wanting to be forgotten. Nick hissed and scampered off into the alley. "Audrey, about Simone—"

"Oh, hi there, big fella!" Audrey said, bending forward to rub the Mastiff's scruff, purposefully ignoring Mason. She didn't want to hear awkward explanations right now about Simone. *Simone.* Was that really her name? It wasn't Tamika, but it was just as exotic. Polpetto leaned into her pets, the big sweetheart, as she lavished her attention on him. "I'm so glad to see you."

"Audrey . . ." Mason's voice was a low murmur.

She didn't raise her eyes to meet his. She couldn't. She didn't want to go there. "I missed you so much!" she said in the baby voice she used with all her animals. "You're such a good boy!"

"Audrey . . ."

"Hmm?" she mumbled, continuing to rub him all over, making his tail wag frantically.

"Audrey!" His voice was almost a bark.

She lifted her eyes to his at once, stunned. When had easygoing Mason ever used that tone of voice with her before. "What?"

"Simone isn't who you think she is."

"Oh?" Audrey asked nonchalantly, sure her face was turning red. It felt hot. "Just who did I think she was?"

"You know," he said, clearly not buying her act. "Yeah, we did go out. But years ago. When I ended it, I thought she got the picture. But I guess not."

Audrey stared in shock for a moment. "Yeah. I guess not."

"Anyway. When you showed up, she'd just gotten here. I told her she had to go, but there were no flights. She didn't have the money for a hotel. But the next day, I made her change her ticket and sent her back to Charleston on the next flight out of Palermo."

"You . . . did?" she stammered, stunned. Polpetto kept wagging his tail, eager for the love, but she'd stopped petting him. "Seriously?"

He smiled, a half-smile that quirked up one side of his mouth. In her chest, her heart felt like it would ignite at any second. She *loved* that smile of his. "Yeah. Of course."

"Why did you do that?" she said, breathless.

He chuckled. "Why do you think?"

Think? What's that? She shook her head slowly. "I . . . don't . . . know?"

He laughed a little more. "You're gonna make me say it out loud? All right," he said, pausing for effect before looking up and down the street. "I've got a thing for you, Boston."

"You . . . do?"

He came down the step so that they were standing on the same level, and gently nudged Polpetto back into the house, so they were

160

alone. "Don't act so surprised. You're damn adorable. And I'm glad you're back. I missed you."

"You . . . did?" she mouthed, now aware that her mouth was hanging open. How long had that been going on for? She clamped it closed. "I mean . . . oh. I'm glad to be back. And yes. I missed you, too."

"You think you might want to go out to dinner with me? This weekend? Just the two of us?"

Audrey gazed up at him. In the dim orange light from his house, he'd never looked better. *He's asking me out on a date. Mason Legare is asking me out! Wait until I tell Brina!* She forced down the teenage urge inside her to giggle like a little girl and managed a polite, mature nod. "That would be lovely."

"Good. Say . . . eight? Saturday?"

She bobbed her head again. "I'd have to check my schedule, but I think that will work just fine."

He looked behind him. Polpetto was scratching at the door. He opened it and stepped in, still smiling at her. She smiled and stepped off his front stoop, and realized she was still nodding. She tried to stop herself, and managed to, just as she took another step back and hit the building across the street. When had that gotten there?

"See you," she said with a rather goofy wave, then turned and headed in the direction of her house.

Or was it in the direction of her house? Where was she again?

Finally, she managed to find her way. By the time she got to her front doorstep, the shock had faded, replaced by outright excitement. Nessa's cameras were out there, recording again, but this time, she didn't care.

She jumped up and down and squealed as loud as she could into the quiet Sicilian night.

*

The following day, Audrey woke up bright and early to get a few hours of work in on the house before heading the clinic. As nice as it would have been, no fairies had broken into *Piazza Tre* while she was gone to fix the place up, so the living room, and its holey walls, were still waiting for her when she got back.

Now, though, she was energized to do the work. And she was excited to call some contractors and possibly see if they could help her speed things up, with the cash she'd gotten from the Lipari trip. She grinned goofily as she spread the spackle on another divot in the plaster and smoothed it out. Maybe that was Mason's effect. Probably, it was. As tired as she'd been, she hadn't slept all night. Instead, she'd kept thinking about the way he'd smiled at her. *I have a thing for you, Boston.*

How cute was that? And he'd called *her* adorable. *Damn* adorable. Insane!

She finished smoothing out the spackle, her phone buzzed with a text from Brina. Of course, she'd had to text her last night, just to spill the tea.

Brina's response made Audrey burst out with laughter. *OMG! But . . . why no more pictures of his abs?*

Audrey shook her head. Brina and her obsession with Mason's abs. Yes, Mason loved to parade around shirtless, and he had every reason to, but the fact was, he didn't need to. There was so much about him that Audrey loved, it made her insides flutter, just thinking about him. And now . . . now they were finally going to go on their first real date. Of course Simone was nobody to him. Mason was a good, decent guy. He'd never two-time her.

Just then, a shriek came from outside.

Alarmed, Audrey ran to the picture window in the living room and threw open the enormous shutters to find Nessa standing in her doorway, leaning against the jamb. She studied her fingernails before giving Audrey a cool look. "Just wanted to see how you liked it," she said.

Audrey looked around. The film crew was already there, setting things up. "What are you talking about?"

"I'm talking about the godawful shriek you made last night. Some people have to sleep, you know! I had to get up at five this morning for makeup!" she complained, fluffing her perfectly curled tendrils. "We have a full day of filming . . .by the way, where were you?"

"In Lipari. I was helping with—"

She waved Audrey away, bored. "No clue where that even is. But I don't care. Could you try to leave the shutters on your place closed? Your mess is interfering with the ambience on the street. Okay?"

"With pleasure," Audrey said, smiling sweetly. Even Nessa's constant complaints couldn't bother her now.

Nessa brought her cell phone to her ear. She started to speak loudly. "Yeah? Talk to me."

Audrey began to pull the shutters closed when Nessa suddenly said, "Montagnanera? Where's that?"

Audrey slowed. *Montagnanera.* The place where her father might be. She'd bought that ticket over a month ago, but since then, kept putting it off. At this rate, she'd never have the time.

But maybe this was a sign. I sign that she needed to go there and check it out, sooner rather than later.

Nessa said, "You know what? Forget it. I don't care. So they're coming here? They bought the place where? Oh. Outside of town? All right. Keep me posted." A pause. "Yeah. Whatever. Later."

Audrey closed the shutters fully and locked them, then went back to the work she was doing on the wall. Yes, her father had been gone from her life for almost twenty years. But not a day went by that she didn't wonder where he was, why he'd left, and if she'd ever see him again. Maybe it was time to stop wondering. Maybe, if she just took that flight, she'd finally know for sure.

I'd have to make sure Concetta is comfortable handling the clinic. I can't leave again right away. But in another few months . . . Hmm. . . who knows? Depending on how well this date goes, maybe Mason would want to come with me?

Her mind whirled with the ideas. She imagined herself walking down a volcanic-sand beach like the one in Lipari, hand-in-hand with Mason, and shivered with excitement.

She'd lived thirty-five years of her life alone. Maybe this time, she'd finally found the one.

She'd just scooped some spackle onto the putty knife when there came a knock at the door. Setting the tool down, she went to the door and pulled it open, expecting to find one of Nessa's camera crewmen, telling her she needed to fix something on her house "for the camera."

But it wasn't anyone from the camera crew.

It was G, the café owner. *"Buonosera, Principessa."*

"G?" she said, confused, as he smiled up at her. "Hey! How are you?"

"I have not seen you in a long time," he said earnestly, giving her his charming smile. "And I was missing you."

"You were?" She grinned. G was such a charmer. Though he was handsome and had a way with people, Audrey had learned not to take him all that seriously. After all, she'd been on many of what she'd thought were "dates" with G, only to have him constantly put the brakes on. He'd never made a move on her. Oh, he'd hug her, but he likely hugged *everyone*. He was just a friendly guy, with a warm, larger-than-life, Sicilian personality. "That's very nice of you. How sweet. I missed you, too."

His brow knitted, and for the first time, Audrey saw something other than joy on his tanned, attractive face. "No . . . I meant that I missed you. Audrey . . ."

She stared at him, confused. What other meaning could there be? "I know . . ."

"When you no come around no more, I think maybe I did something wrong?" he asked, pulling off his skull cap and holding it in his hands, revealing his closely trimmed dark hair.

"Oh, no. Not at all. Didn't anyone tell you?" He had so many friends, it seemed odd that he wouldn't have heard. "I was in Lip—"

"I know. I heard that. But I thought you left maybe because I did something that made you mad?" he asked. "After that night, all those weeks ago . . . with the desserts, you have not been happy with me. I see. I did something wrong."

That night? Audrey blinked. It had been so long ago, she barely thought of it now. Yes, she'd been upset. She'd wanted a romantic evening alone, and then he'd gone and invited his friends. But after that—

"And the night we went to dinner. You'd wanted something. And I did not deliver."

Her eyes widened. Yes. She'd been a little tipsy. And she'd stared up into his eyes, getting lost in them. She'd been overcome with the cool night air, and the magic of the full moon, and a little bit of desperation, too. She'd wanted . . .

Oh no.

He took a step forward.

She took a step back.

He sighed, and started to rub the back of his neck anxiously. "I am sorry, *Principessa.* You see, I am not very good where beautiful women are concerned. I missed a grand opportunity, and I've thought of it every night since. How I have failed you. So I ask you—no, I beg you—to please forgive me? To give me another chance?"

He bowed his head humbly.

Audrey clasped at her heart. Was this really happening?

"Uh . . . *sure?*" she said, not really certain that this was actually happening. This past twenty-four hours, with Mason, and now G? It had to be some kind of dream. This wasn't her life.

G grinned broadly, hopefully, and suddenly lunged forward and grabbed both of her hands. He kissed them, again and again and again, until she really wished he was pinching her, so that she could wake up.

"*Principessa!*" he shouted, like she'd made him the happiest man on earth. "Let us go out this weekend!"

"Well . . . actually . . ." Audrey started.

"*Venerdì!* I will treat you like the beautiful princess you are."

She looked down at Nick, who gave her a look like, *This is a fine mess you've gotten yourself into.* But really, Audrey knew, it wouldn't be her life unless it was complicated. She'd just have to figure things out like she always did.

And hope that she didn't break anyone's heart in the process . . . including her own.

NOW AVAILABLE!

A VILLA IN SICILY: ORANGE GROVES AND VENGEANCE
(A Cats and Dogs Cozy Mystery—Book 5)

"Very entertaining. Highly recommended for the permanent library of any reader who appreciates a well-written mystery with twists and an intelligent plot. You will not be disappointed. Excellent way to spend a cold weekend!"
--Books and Movie Reviews (regarding *Murder in the Manor*)

A VILLA IN SICILY: ORANGE GROVES AND VENGEANCE is book #5 in a charming new cozy mystery series by bestselling author Fiona Grace, author of *Murder in the Manor*, a #1 Bestseller with over 100 five-star reviews (and a free download)!

Audrey Smart, 34, has made a major life change, walking away from her life as a vet (and from a string of failed romances) and moving to Sicily to buy a $1 home—and embark on a mandatory renovation she knows nothing about. She finds herself busy running the town's new shelter, while also renovating her own problematic home—and dating again.

When Audrey gets a call to find an injured stray in an orange grove at an old estate, the last thing she expects to find is love. The estate owner is charming, handsome—and like no one she's met before. Might he be a Mafiosi?

It seems like the surprises never end, until she finds one more thing on her way out of the grove: a dead body.

A laugh-out-loud cozy packed with mystery, intrigue, renovation, animals, food, wine—and of course, love—A VILLA IN SICILY will capture your heart and keep you glued to the very last page.

Book #6 in the series—CANNOLI AND A CASUALTY—is now also available!

Fiona Grace

Fiona Grace is author of the LACEY DOYLE COZY MYSTERY series, comprising nine books; of the TUSCAN VINEYARD COZY MYSTERY series, comprising seven books; of the DUBIOUS WITCH COZY MYSTERY series, comprising three books; of the BEACHFRONT BAKERY COZY MYSTERY series, comprising six books; and of the CATS AND DOGS COZY MYSTERY series, comprising nine books.

Fiona would love to hear from you, so please visit www.fionagraceauthor.com to receive free ebooks, hear the latest news, and stay in touch.

BOOKS BY FIONA GRACE

LACEY DOYLE COZY MYSTERY
MURDER IN THE MANOR (Book#1)
DEATH AND A DOG (Book #2)
CRIME IN THE CAFE (Book #3)
VEXED ON A VISIT (Book #4)
KILLED WITH A KISS (Book #5)
PERISHED BY A PAINTING (Book #6)
SILENCED BY A SPELL (Book #7)
FRAMED BY A FORGERY (Book #8)
CATASTROPHE IN A CLOISTER (Book #9)

TUSCAN VINEYARD COZY MYSTERY
AGED FOR MURDER (Book #1)
AGED FOR DEATH (Book #2)
AGED FOR MAYHEM (Book #3)
AGED FOR SEDUCTION (Book #4)
AGED FOR VENGEANCE (Book #5)
AGED FOR ACRIMONY (Book #6)
AGED FOR MALICE (Book #7)

DUBIOUS WITCH COZY MYSTERY
SKEPTIC IN SALEM: AN EPISODE OF MURDER (Book #1)
SKEPTIC IN SALEM: AN EPISODE OF CRIME (Book #2)
SKEPTIC IN SALEM: AN EPISODE OF DEATH (Book #3)

BEACHFRONT BAKERY COZY MYSTERY
BEACHFRONT BAKERY: A KILLER CUPCAKE (Book #1)
BEACHFRONT BAKERY: A MURDEROUS MACARON (Book #2)
BEACHFRONT BAKERY: A PERILOUS CAKE POP (Book #3)
BEACHFRONT BAKERY: A DEADLY DANISH (Book #4)
BEACHFRONT BAKERY: A TREACHEROUS TART (Book #5)
BEACHFRONT BAKERY: A CALAMITOUS COOKIE (Book #6)

CATS AND DOGS COZY MYSTERY
A VILLA IN SICILY: OLIVE OIL AND MURDER (Book #1)
A VILLA IN SICILY: FIGS AND A CADAVER (Book #2)
A VILLA IN SICILY: VINO AND DEATH (Book #3)
A VILLA IN SICILY: CAPERS AND CALAMITY (Book #4)

Made in United States
North Haven, CT
23 January 2022

15128482R00105